SPIDER-MAN 3

THE JUNIOR NOVEL

COLUMBIA PICTURES PRESENTS A MARVEL STUDIOS/LAURA ZISKIN PRODUCTION A SAM RAIMI FILM TOBEY MAGUIRE "SPIDER-MAN 3" KIRSTEN DUNST JAMES FRANCO THOMAS HADEN CHURCH TOPHER GRACE BRYCE DALLAS HOWARD MUSIC BY DANNY ELFMAN SCORE BY CHRISTOPHER YOUNG EXECUTIVE PRODUCERS STAN LEE KEVIN FEIGE JOSEPH M. CARACCIOLO BASED ON THE MARVEL COMIC BOOK BY STAN LEE AND STEVE DITKO

MARVEL SPIDER-MAN CHARACTER TM & © 2006 MARVEL CHARACTERS, INC. ALL RIGHTS RESERVED. STORY BY SAM RAIMI & IVAN RAIMI SCREENPLAY BY ALVIN SARGENT PRODUCED BY LAURA ZISKIN AVI ARAD GRANT CURTIS DIRECTED BY SAM RAIMI COLUMBIA PICTURES

sony.com/Spider-Man

Library of Congress catalog card number: 2006934362
ISBN-10: 0-06-083725-X — ISBN-13: 978-0-06-083725-9

Book design by John Sazaklis
❖

SPIDER-MAN 3

THE JUNIOR NOVEL

By Jasmine Jones

Screenplay by Alvin Sargent

Screen Story by Sam Raimi & Ivan Raimi

Based on the Marvel Comic Book by Stan Lee and Steve Ditko

📚 HarperEntertainment
An Imprint of HarperCollinsPublishers

CHAPTER 1

The bright neon lights of Times Square flashed on and off. Swarms of people hurried this way and that, rushing to different theaters for an evening of entertainment. Peter Parker smiled to himself as he worked his way through the crowd. He was off to the theater, too. He stopped short when a little boy ran in front of him. The kid was wearing a Spider-Man T-shirt, and he grinned up at Peter, and then looked beyond him to the buildings above. Following his gaze, Peter saw a scrolling billboard. NEW YORK, it flashed, ♥'S SPIDER-MAN!

Peter couldn't help but feel ecstatic. For the first time in his life, Peter felt popular. *Well,* he thought, *I'm popular as Spider-Man, anyway.* Even if he didn't make a lot of money as a freelance photographer and didn't live in the greatest apartment, he knew his alter ego was loved in New York. And that was enough to keep him happy.

As Peter walked toward the theater at the end of the street, he passed several kids dressed as Spider-Man. Peter knew that the kids of the city admired him—they wanted to be just like him. After all, he was a hero. The people of New York City were safe and sound, and Peter knew he was directly responsible for that. *Criminals don't stand a chance in this city,* Peter thought. Uncle Ben would be so proud of him.

Peter felt a painful twinge at the thought of Uncle Ben. It had been a few years since his uncle's death, but the memory of his murder was still fresh in Peter's mind. Peter had found the killer and brought him to justice, but he still missed his uncle every day. But Peter knew that his uncle would have liked the fact that he had accepted his responsibility as Spider-Man. "With great power comes great responsibility."—Uncle Ben had always loved that saying. Peter had learned that his gifts were for fighting crime and protecting the citizens of New York. And he fulfilled those duties every single day.

Even though most people loved him as Spider-Man, Peter was doing pretty well as himself. On top of all his crime fighting, he still managed to get to school every day. In fact, he was ranked at the top of his class.

Even better, Peter was in love. He thought about Mary Jane, his childhood sweetheart, as he stood outside the theater where she was performing that night. Peter couldn't believe it—he finally had the girl.

He looked up at the marquee advertising the show. It was Mary Jane's opening night on Broadway. *She's finally made it*, Peter said to himself. This was a huge night for her.

Life is good, he thought. *Life is really good*.

Peter paused a moment to straighten his tie before trailing into the elegant theater lobby along with the buzzing crowd. Nearby was a life-sized poster featuring a beautiful, smiling Mary Jane. MARY JANE WATSON IN *MANHATTAN MEMORIES*! touted the poster. It was a musical, and Mary Jane had the lead role.

This is the part she's always dreamed of, Peter thought. He couldn't believe that his girl-friend was the star. Everything in his life was per-fect. Or *almost* perfect. All that was missing was Harry Osborn. Harry and Peter had been best friends for as long as either one could remember. But Harry's father, the rich and powerful Norman Osborn, had gone insane and terrorized New York City as the Green Goblin. The Green Goblin died in a fight with Spider-Man. And when Harry found out that Peter was Spider-Man, he couldn't forgive him. Harry didn't want to accept that his father had been sick—that he had wanted to hurt Spider-Man and the rest of the people in the city. He just wanted to believe that Peter was cruel.

The lights dimmed as Peter took his seat in the front row. The orchestra struck up a happy tune as Mary Jane appeared onstage. The audience clapped at her appearance. Peter felt the excitement running through the crowd, or maybe that was just the excitement running through Mary Jane. She looked gorgeous, and as she started the first song, Peter felt as though she was singing just for him. The words flew out to him like gentle kisses.

For the entire length of the show, Peter felt like he was in a dream. He had never been so happy in his life.

Peter was impressed by Mary Jane's performance. *She was great*, he thought to himself as he left the theater. Even though his opinion was slightly biased, Peter had to believe that other people had liked the musical as much as he had. Maybe the applause hadn't been as loud as he had expected. And maybe nobody—nobody but Peter—had stood to give Mary Jane an ovation when she came out to take her curtain call, but that didn't matter. She was great!

When Peter walked out of the theater, he spotted a familiar face in the crowd. It was Harry

Osborn. Peter knew he needed to explain to Harry how his father died. He had tried to see Harry at the offices of OsCorp, the enormous company that Harry had inherited from his father, but Harry had instructed the receptionist not to let Peter past her desk.

Still, Peter just couldn't give up on his old friend. He missed Harry. He wished he could find a way to explain that he *hadn't* killed the Green Goblin—it had been an accident. "Harry!" Peter called, as his friend stepped into the backseat of his glossy black Town Car. "Harry, wait! Don't keep locking me out." Peter gazed at his oldest friend through the car window. "You need to hear the truth."

Harry felt a pull at his heart. Peter *was* his closest friend. Perhaps he should hear him out.

Suddenly, Norman Osborn's face appeared in the car window. His father's chiseled features were fierce with disapproval. "Don't weaken," he said to his son.

"I'm your friend," Peter went on, unable to see the reflection of Norman Osborn, glaring at him from the window. "Your father was my friend."

Harry cast a glance at his father's image.

"Don't weaken," Norman Osborn growled.

Harry signaled to his driver. Without a word, he drove away, leaving Peter alone at the curb. The taillights faded into the distance, blending into the rest of the traffic that swirled up the busy avenue.

"Peter," Mary Jane said warmly as Peter joined her backstage. She was standing in the doorway to her dressing room, still wearing her costume from the show. Around them, people chatted in the narrow hallway.

Mary Jane wrapped him in a hug. "Was I good?" Her voice was eager and hopeful, and her green eyes shone brightly.

"Good?" Peter beamed. "You were *great*."

Mary Jane blushed slightly, giving her lovely face a rosy glow. Taking Peter by the hand, she led him into her dressing room and shut the door. Two vases stood on her vanity table. Peter recognized the smaller bouquet as the bunch he'd had delivered. A behemoth arrangement towered beside his smaller one, making it look tiny.

"I got your flowers," Mary Jane chirped, tossing her long red hair over her shoulder as she bustled around to change out of her costume. "Thank you. They're beautiful. And these are from Harry." She gestured toward the gargantuan blossoms. "Was he here tonight?"

Peter sighed and shook his head. "I saw him, but he wouldn't talk to me."

"I'm so sorry." Mary Jane's voice was gentle as she grabbed her coat and led Peter back into the hall. "What is it with you guys, anyway?"

"It's complicated," Peter said. Even though Mary Jane knew that Peter was Spider-Man, he hadn't explained exactly what had happened between himself and Norman Osborn.

An elegantly dressed older gentleman moved toward the exit. He hesitated before speaking to Mary Jane, but after a moment, it became clear that he couldn't get to the door without passing her. "Congratulations, my dear," he said stiffly. "You were quite good."

Mary Jane looked like she might faint from joy

as the man passed through the doorway. "He won a Tony Award," she whispered to Peter as the older gentleman walked away. "He liked me!" she said deliriously. "I think I'm happy." She grabbed Peter by the arm. "Let's celebrate."

Peter grinned. "I've got my bike," he said. He knew just where to take Mary Jane.

The wind whipped through Mary Jane's hair as she and Peter sped out of Manhattan on his motorbike. She clung to his back as they rode over a bridge and out into the country. Mary Jane breathed in the fresh air. It was nice to get out of the city every now and then. Even though she loved the excitement and all of the hustle and bustle, sometimes she liked the quiet, too.

Once they found a perfect spot between two trees, Peter created a web hammock, and the two lay on their backs to look up at the stars. Overhead, a meteor shower sparkled against the inky sky, as though it was raining starlight.

"You know what?" Mary Jane said dreamily

as she watched the meteors dance across the sky. "I'd like to sing on the stage for the rest of my life, with you in the front row." She had been nervous before the show, but once she had seen Peter in the audience, all of her fears faded away. He was the one she was singing for, after all.

"I'll be there," Peter promised. He couldn't think of anything he would like more.

"Tell me you love me." Mary Jane nestled against Peter's shoulder and looked up into his large blue eyes. "I like to hear it. It makes me feel safe."

"I will always love you, Mary Jane," Peter said. It didn't sound silly or mushy, either. It just sounded like the truth, which it was. "I always have."

They were so happy together, lying there, looking up at the stars, that neither one noticed the small black rock that hissed on the other side of a nearby field. The meteorite was hot from crashing through the Earth's atmosphere. As smoke rose from the rock, something dark oozed from inside the stone. It slithered across the grass like a snake. Moving toward Peter and Mary Jane, it slid onto Peter's bike and stayed there, waiting. . . .

CHAPTER 2

Flint Marko hurried down the alley, clutching a stack of rubber-banded letters. He knew that he had to get out of his prison uniform as quickly as possible. The police were after him, and the uniform was a dead giveaway that he had just escaped.

Flint grunted as he grabbed a striped sweater from a nearby laundry line, then a pair of pants. He changed quickly, dumped his old prison jumpsuit into a garbage can, and skulked into the shadows as a police cruiser drove past.

With one swift jump, he grabbed a fire escape ladder and started to climb. He stopped at a window and peered in. A nine-year-old girl was asleep inside, her face half-hidden in the darkness. Opening the window softly, Flint climbed into her room and eyed the piggy bank on her dresser. Then, with gentle hands, he tucked the stack of letters under her pillow. They were the letters he had written to the little girl when he was in prison. This was his daughter, Penny. And all of these letters had been returned to him unopened. Flint knew that his wife, Emma, had been responsible for that. She was furious at him for breaking the law and going to jail. Flint didn't blame her for feeling that way. But he never meant for things to turn out the way they did. He'd just been trying to get some money. His family needed it, and he didn't know how else to get it.

As quiet as a cat, Flint slipped into the dark kitchen and pulled the lid off the cookie jar. He reached in, took out a handful of cash, and slipped it into his pocket.

The light clicked on, and Flint Marko blinked at

the sudden appearance of his wife.

He held up his hands in surrender. "I'm just here to see my daughter."

"Get out of here," Emma spat. Her face was twisted in anger. "You're guilty, Marko. Guilty as sin."

"I want to do good," Flint said calmly. "That's the truth."

"I live in the presence of great truth," Emma shot back, gesturing to Penny's room. "That's the truth you left behind. Right there in that bedroom." Both Emma and Flint knew that Penny was sick—very sick—and neither one of them could afford her medical bills. But if money had been tight before Flint went to jail, it was even scarcer now.

"I am not bad," Flint insisted. "I had bad luck—that's different."

Penny appeared in the doorway. She looked up at her father with huge eyes, and gave him a locket. He looked down at the silver heart in his hand. It was still warm from lying against her skin.

"Now get out!" Emma shouted as sirens wailed

in the distance. The police were on their way. "Get out! You're always hiding, climbing in and out of windows. You'll end up where you belong, crawling on the ground, as useless as a grain of sand."

Flint headed for the nearest window. "I want to do good. That's the truth." He stopped for a moment, his eyes lingering on his daughter. "Pray for me," he said as he ducked out.

Emma wrapped Penny in a tight hug. Penny had woken up and found her father's letters. She was still holding them, but she hid them from her mother's sight. She knew that her mother wouldn't want her to have them. But Penny still loved her father, even though she knew that he had done some bad things. He still did bad things, sometimes. "He took my piggy bank," Penny told her mother.

Aunt May blinked wearily as she wrapped her robe tight over her nightgown and stumbled across the floor of her apartment. *Why on earth would someone be banging on my door at two o'clock in the morning?* she wondered as she stopped in the foyer. "Who is it?" she asked.

"Peter!" yelled an excited voice.

Aunt May pulled open the door. Her nephew, Peter, stood there, his wide blue eyes shining over an enormous grin. He looked like someone who was about to burst with news. "I've decided to marry Mary Jane," he announced.

Aunt May's hand fluttered to her throat. Of all of the things that her nephew could have said, this was the most unexpected. And when the unexpected strikes, there is only one thing to do. "This calls for a cup of tea," Aunt May said.

Peter looked around Aunt May's cozy kitchen. It wasn't as nice as the one she used to have, before hard times forced her to move out of the house she had shared with Uncle Ben. Peter had felt horrible when he found out Aunt May was being evicted. He felt that he should have been able to earn enough money to help her. In the end, though, there was nothing that either of them could do. The new apartment was decent, and Aunt May kept it tidy. Peter tried hard not to miss the old place too much.

At least the tea is the same, Peter thought as he sipped from his cup.

Aunt May sighed as she remembered the night Uncle Ben first asked her to marry him. "We were both scared and excited and very young," she told Peter. "And I loved him so fiercely."

"And you said yes," Peter prompted. "Right?"

Aunt May shook her head. "No," she said slowly. "I wasn't ready." She looked her nephew in the eye. "Love is not enough, Peter. There's so much more beyond it that has to be considered. You need a steady job."

Peter thought this over. Aunt May was right. If he wanted to start a family with Mary Jane, he needed more money than he had. He could hardly even afford his own apartment, much less an engagement ring!

Almost as though she had read his thoughts, Aunt May pulled the diamond ring from her own finger and placed it in Peter's palm. She remembered well what it was like to be young and in love—and she knew how much Peter loved Mary Jane. "I hope you've considered a proper proposal," she said to him.

Peter smiled. To tell the truth, he had spent a lot of time thinking about the proposal. He knew just what he would say. And now that he had a ring and Aunt May's blessing, he would go ahead and do it.

All he needed was a better job, like Aunt May said. With benefits.

Peter knew that the *Daily Bugle* was looking for a full-time staff photographer—they had already run an advertisement. *I wonder if I could get that job,* he thought. Peter had been working there as a freelance photographer, and got paid whenever the editor-in-chief—J. Jonah Jameson—decided he liked one of Peter's photos. That was fairly often, given that Peter was the only person in the city who had managed to take a photo of Spider-Man.

If I had a staff position, I'd get paid a salary, Peter thought. *A steady paycheck every week. Plus benefits.*

That was it. He'd have to get a staff job at the *Bugle.* One way or another, Peter decided, he would.

CHAPTER 3

Deep within the Green Goblin's lair, gas hissed inside the Strength-Enhancing Chamber. Through the glass windows that enclosed him, Harry could see the weapons— pumpkin bombs, silver armor, the jet-powered Sky-Stick. He still had all of the weapons that his father had used . . . and he had a few new ones that Norman Osborn had never had a chance to try. Harry breathed in the Strength-Enhancing Gas. *Once I'm finished with this treatment,* Harry thought, *I'll be able to take on Spider-Man. I'll get* *revenge for what he did to my father.*

Norman Osborn often spoke to his son through reflections and mirrors, telling him what to do. And he wanted Harry to kill Spider-Man.

The hissing stopped, and Harry stepped out of the chamber. Energy coursed through his veins— he felt like a new man. Stronger, faster, more powerful than ever before. He was the New Goblin.

And he would make his father proud.

Peter Parker waited in the newsroom to talk to his boss, J. Jonah Jameson. He was nervous, but excited, too. After all, if he got the staff job, he'd be able to propose to Mary Jane right away!

The editor-in-chief bellowed behind the door of his office. Peter looked over at J.J.'s assistant, who rolled her eyes. J.J. was known for blowing a fuse over the smallest thing. He'd been in a foul mood ever since Spider-Man saved the city from Doc Ock. Now that crime was down, there were fewer stories about the hero in the paper, which meant that people weren't buying as many copies of the *Daily Bugle*. That left J.J.

with a perpetual bad temper.

To make things even worse, another photographer, named Eddie Brock, also wanted the full-time job. He had photographs of Spider-Man, too. Eddie got into Mr. Jameson's office first, which was bad news for Peter. Talking about money always made J.J. furious. By the time Peter was able to talk to J. J., the boss was in a rage. When Peter asked for more money, too, he hit the roof!

"You're not the only photographer in town!" J.J. shouted.

Peter ducked out of there. Clearly he hadn't picked the best moment to talk to his boss.

I'll just have to try again later, he thought.

Disappointed, Peter made his way down the street, away from the office. *I'll find a way to get that job*, he promised himself. *I have to get that job. For Mary Jane—*

All of a sudden Peter was hit by something full force, and he found himself soaring into the air. It was the Goblin! He had attacked Peter, and both were rocketing upward on the Goblin's Sky-Stick!

The ground fell away as they soared higher, higher.

It can't be! Peter thought, his eyes wild with shock. His mind whirled. The Green Goblin was dead—Peter had seen the body with his own eyes; he had even gone to the funeral. But there was no doubt that he was here, now, riding a Sky-Stick. *This must be someone else,* Peter reasoned. Someone dressed as the Green Goblin—a New Goblin!

The New Goblin tightened his grip on Peter. The Strength-Enhancing Gas had worked. He was stronger and faster than ever before! And he could tell that Peter was shocked by his appearance. *The element of surprise,* Harry thought, smiling beneath his mask.

The New Goblin yanked Peter's hair, pulling his head back so that his throat was exposed. With a metallic clink, blades sprouted from the villain's armor. *This is my moment!* the New Goblin thought triumphantly. *The moment in which I avenge my father!*

Wind whipped past Peter's exposed neck as they shot into the sky. It didn't matter who this

New Goblin was or where he had come from. Peter knew he had to do something—fast.

Grabbing the New Goblin's arm, Peter kicked at his chest, then flipped himself over—and out of the villain's grip. He fired a web at his opponent.

Slice!

The New Goblin cut through the web, but Peter had managed to cling to the side of a building. He looked down. He couldn't believe what he saw. The web had knocked the New Goblin's mask open, revealing his face.

Peter's mouth dropped open. "Harry?"

"Face it, Pete," Harry snarled. "It had to come to this."

"I didn't kill your father," Peter insisted.

"Shut up!" Harry's voice was a roar as he fired a cruel blast at Peter.

Boom!

Chunks of brick and mortar flew apart right where Peter had been clinging only a moment before. *He really wants me dead!* Peter realized as he leaped away. With the speed of a spider, he crawled from building to building, hurrying down the wide street and ducking into a narrow alley. As long as he was in the open, the New Goblin had the advantage. He could fly in the open air, while Spider-Man had to cling to the sides of buildings. In a smaller space, though, it would be harder for the New Goblin to maneuver. And Spider-Man could use his skills.

Looking back, Peter could see that Harry was still gaining on him. He slung a web to make a trip wire, and Harry hit it at full speed. He was torn from his Sky-Stick, and fell, screaming, into the alley below.

Oh, no! Peter thought as he gazed down at his friend's body, which lay in a twisted heap near the end of the alley. He hurried to his friend's side. Harry was hurt. Badly.

Peter gathered him in his arms and carried him to the hospital emergency room.

Flint Marko raced through a marsh outside of the city. He was in New Jersey, running from the police. Their flashlights winked behind him in the dark as the sound of barking dogs got closer and closer. "Halt!" cried one of the officers, but Flint didn't halt. He didn't even slow down. He just kept running—he wasn't even sure where he was going.

With a metallic *chink*, Flint collided with a chain-link fence. He didn't stop to read the sign that said, DANGER! HIGH-ENERGY PARTICLE PHYSICS TEST SITE. KEEP OUT! as he climbed over—and fell directly into a massive bowl of sand.

The police would find him soon. *They'll probably be here any minute*, Flint thought as he lay close to the ground. Still, Flint took a moment to pull the small silver locket Penny had given him from his pocket. His heart ached as he looked at it. He missed his daughter with a pain that was almost unbearable. He would have been able to accept his prison sentence if he didn't have to live knowing that his daughter was at home, suffering because he couldn't provide for her. He couldn't take it, and so he had escaped.

Now all he had to do was find a way to help her.

Flint struggled to his feet. But as he stretched, he heard a soft hum. Looking over his shoulder, Flint saw a sleek machine with complex parts. It was a particle-accelerator gun . . . and it was pointed right at him.

With a deafening sound, the gun fired at Flint, covering him in sand particles. The particles had been heated and sped up, so that they were moving at top speed as they spewed across Flint's body.

Flint screamed as the tiny sand crystals shot into his skin. They glowed with a strange light as they merged with his body. As the crystals burned white-hot, his body became one giant mass of sand—it was impossible to tell one tiny grain from another.

By the time the police arrived, there was nothing left but a pile of sand. At the center was the locket that Penny had given her father. It was glowing.

It wasn't easy for Flint Marko to stand up. His legs felt like beanbags beneath him. He rocked back and forth at every step, first nearly falling on his face, next nearly falling on his side. Flint stared at his hand. There was no question about it—he was made of sand.

It made him want to weep, but he couldn't. He was too furious. *Look what they did to me!* he thought. *I'm not even a man anymore! I'm a Sandman.*

But I'm still me, Flint thought. *I'm standing. I'm even . . . walking.*

He pitched to the side and windmilled his arms to keep from falling over. With an enormous effort, Flint hauled his leg forward and took another step. Then he managed another. And another.

I think I'm getting the hang of this, Flint thought as he trudged ahead.

It doesn't matter if I'm made of sand or not, he decided. *Nothing is going to stop me from saving my little girl.*

The next morning, Peter noticed a blob of black goo on his shoe. *That's weird,* he thought, squinting at the strange stuff. *I wonder where I picked that up.* He'd never seen anything like it.

Peter dug around on his side table for a rag,

but when he reached down to wipe the black goo away, it had disappeared. *That's odd,* Peter thought. He scanned the floor, but there was no sign of the gelatinous ooze.

I think I'm seeing things, he said to himself. It wasn't a comforting thought.

Just then, a frantic knock sounded at the door. Peter opened it to see Mary Jane standing there. She didn't give him a smile, didn't even say hello. Instead, she just held up the newspaper she was carrying.

Peter looked at the headline. It wasn't about Spider-Man. *Why is she showing me this?* he wondered. "What?" Peter asked.

"The review," Mary Jane said. Her voice was flat.

"How was it?" Peter asked. "Great?"

"They hated it," Mary Jane said miserably as she trudged into Peter's apartment. "They hated me."

Peter didn't believe it. "You were great," he insisted. *The review probably isn't half as bad as she thinks it is*, he said to himself.

Lifting her delicate eyebrows, Mary Jane turned to the page with the review and started to read. "The young Miss Watson is a pretty girl, easy on the eyes, but not on the ears."

Peter winced. Mary Jane was right—it *wasn't* a very good review. In fact, it was awful. But he didn't understand it—Mary Jane had sounded great to him. "Spider-Man gets attacked all the time," Peter pointed out, trying to be helpful. It was true. J. Jonah Jameson hated Spider-Man. He was always writing editorials criticizing him in the *Daily Bugle*.

"This isn't about you!" Mary Jane slapped the paper on Peter's table. "I'm tired of being pretty."

"It's a critic," Peter pointed out. "These people can be thieves, they can steal our potential. You have to believe in yourself—"

"Try to understand how I feel!" Mary Jane begged. Her eyes watered, and she started to cry. She couldn't help it. She had been so excited about the show, and now it was ruined for her. *How can I perform tonight?* she wondered. *How can I go on, knowing that people out there think I'm lousy?*

A loud siren cut through Mary Jane's sobs. Peter looked over at the police radio. Someone was reporting that a crane was out of control. People were in danger! They needed Spider-Man.

He looked at Mary Jane. She wanted him to stay. She needed him. But other people needed him, too, and without Spider-Man, they could die.

Peter didn't really have a choice. He had to go. He just hoped that Mary Jane could understand.

Gwen Stacy stifled a yawn as she posed for the camera. She was a college student, but she sometimes took modeling jobs to pay the bills. This was one of the more boring assignments— an office-supply catalog. She wished she were back in chemistry class, comparing notes with her friend, Peter Parker. *Do they even* need *people in these photos?* Gwen wondered as she leaned against a metal desk. *Can't they just take nice pictures of the staplers?*

The photographer frowned as a crane appeared in the window behind Gwen. He didn't understand where it had come from—and now it was going to mess up his picture.

Seeing his glance, Gwen looked outside. There

was something about that crane—it looked wobbly. A steel girder hung by a cable below it, and the cable was swinging awfully close to the building. . . .

"Get down!" Gwen screamed as the girder shattered the window. It crashed into the lighting fixtures in the studio, tearing them down. Then the crane slammed back out the window. Glass fell like rain over everything in the room as the lights flickered and went out.

"It's coming back!" the photographer shouted a moment before the crane toppled. There was a smashing *crunch* as it knocked out the columns on the floor below their own.

Gwen felt dizzy as the ground beneath her shifted, tilted, and then dropped away. She let out a scream as she slid across the floor. Flailing wildly, she reached for something—anything to keep her from plunging to the street below. But the only thing her hand caught was a telephone. Gwen stopped at the edge of the broken window when the cord pulled tight, but then the cord snapped and in the next moment she was falling again. She grabbed onto the window frame and clung there, one hundred stories above the pavement.

Pop! Pop!

The rivets that held the window in place gave way, and the metal bar she'd grabbed on to swung away from the side of the building, high over a busy intersection.

She couldn't hold on—her fingers were slipping.

Gwen let out a scream as she fell . . . right into the arms of Spider-Man! She held on to him tightly. She had never been so happy to see anyone in her entire life.

"Does it ever lose its thrill?" she asked Spider-Man as he swung her away from the collapsing building.

Spider-Man seemed caught off guard. "Well, after a while . . ." he began, but stopped. He thought for a moment. "Actually, it's still really cool."

Down on the street below, Eddie Brock snapped a photo of Spider-Man and the beautiful girl in his arms. "My God," Eddie said to himself, "that's Gwen!" It had taken him a moment to recognize his girlfriend through the camera lens.

The police captain by his side was dumbfounded. "That's my daughter," he cried. "What was she doing up there?"

A shattering *clang* echoed through the city as the police managed to cut the electricity on the block and shut down the crane. Eddie introduced himself to Captain Stacy. He explained that Gwen had a modeling job in the office building that afternoon. Brock continued snapping pictures as Spider-Man deposited Gwen safely on the sidewalk.

"Beautiful," Eddie said as he took another photo. "Pulitzer Prize." He smirked as he held up the camera. "Wait till you see the shot, Gwen. You okay?"

Gwen managed a shaky smile. "I'm fine, Eddie." She didn't really think of Eddie as her boyfriend. They'd only had one date, after all. But she knew that Eddie felt differently, and that made her uncomfortable.

Eddie held out his hand to Spider-Man. "I'm new," he explained when he saw Spider-Man looking at his press badge. DAILY BUGLE, it read. "Eddie Brock. I'll be taking shots of you for the paper from now on."

Spider-Man was taken off guard by this news. He asked where Peter Parker was, even though—of course—he already knew the answer. Eddie assured him that he was the new official Spider-Man photographer.

That's just what I was afraid of, Peter thought, his expression hidden beneath his mask.

CHAPTER 4

A short while later, Eddie walked into J.J. Jameson's office with his photo of Spider-Man rescuing Gwen from the collapsing building. J.J. loved it. Although he wasn't a fan of the webbed wonder, he always loved having an exciting photo of the hero on his front page. And this new kid, Eddie—he worked for cheap! J.J. was about to pay him when Peter Parker hurried into his office with his own photo of Spider-Man.

The editor-in-chief puzzled over the two shots. They were both good. He couldn't decide which was better. He usually didn't have this problem—no one but Peter had ever been able to get a photo of Spider-Man. In the end, though, he had to admit that Eddie's was slightly better. It had a lot of drama, and the lighting was perfect. The colors in Brock's photo were really rich. J.J. Jameson made his choice—he went with Eddie's picture.

Peter was disappointed, but he wasn't about to give up. He wanted that staff job, and he believed he had earned it. The trouble was, Eddie wanted the job, too, and he let J.J. know.

But J.J. Jameson didn't care which photographer got the job. They were all the same to him. All he wanted was to sell newspapers.

And one other thing.

"I want the public to see Spider-Man for the two-bit criminal he really is." J.J. snarled. "He's a fake. Catch him in the act." The editor smiled at the thought. A photo of Spider-Man committing a crime—that would sell a million copies!

"Spider-Man with his hand in the cookie jar. Whoever brings me that photo gets the job."

Peter left his boss's office feeling dejected. He knew there was no way he'd ever get that photo. Uncle Ben's voice rang in his ears: "With great power comes great responsibility." Uncle Ben had always liked that quote. Peter knew that he would never dishonor his uncle's memory by putting his powers to the wrong use.

Spider-Man wasn't a crook. And he wasn't going to become one just so Peter could get a job.

Peter held open the door for his best friend as Harry stepped gingerly into the front hallway of his magnificent home. An enormous spray of fresh flowers filled a beautiful vase. The hallway was paneled with rich, dark wood, and elegant Oriental carpets lined the floors. Harry looked around, blinking slowly, as his butler greeted him.

"Thank God you're all right," Bernard said. He had worked for Norman Osborn for years, and had known Harry since he was a small child. But Harry looked confused. He could tell that

Bernard was a butler, but he didn't remember anything about him. When Harry had woken up in the hospital, he realized that he didn't remember much. His horrible fall from the Sky-Stick had wiped out much of his recent memory. In fact, he didn't even remember that he was now the New Goblin . . . or that his best friend, Peter, was Spider-Man.

Naturally, that was wonderful news for Peter. Not only was his best friend alive and well, all Harry remembered was that he and Peter were pals and had been for many years. It meant Peter had his friend back—and he didn't have to worry about fighting the New Goblin. He was so thrilled that Harry was coming home that he brought him a present. Peter hadn't wanted to give Harry the gift at the hospital, so he had held on to it on the ride home. Now he presented the round, awkwardly-wrapped package. Peter had a lot of superpowers—but giftwrapping wasn't one of them.

Harry ripped off the paper and pulled out a worn orange basketball. "It's your old ball.

Thanks, buddy." He dribbled it slowly against the wood floor a couple of times, as though he was remembering how. Then looked up at his best friend. "Do I have a girlfriend?" he asked Peter.

A smile flickered on his lips as Peter shook his head in surprise. "I don't know," he said truthfully. After all, it had been a while since he and Harry had had a heart-to-heart. He didn't think Harry had a girlfriend. But he was rich and handsome . . . *Come to think of it,* Peter mused, *why doesn't Harry have a girlfriend?*

Harry glanced around his lavish home, then shot the ball at Peter, who caught it. "It looks like I'm not hurting for money," Harry said.

Peter laughed as he twirled the ball in his hands. "Harry, you're loaded." Norman Osborn had been the owner of the multimillion-dollar OsCorp, the company that had manufactured all of his Green Goblin gear. It was a high-tech firm with holdings all over the world, and Harry had inherited it when his father died. Harry was *more* than loaded.

Slowly, Harry walked toward the life-sized portrait

of his father. Posed stiffly in formal clothes, Norman glared down at his son from the height of the tall canvas. "I wish I could remember more about him," Harry said sadly.

Peter pressed his lips together. *You have no idea how happy I am that you can't,* he thought. "He loved you. That's the main thing." He tossed the ball back at his friend, but it took a strange hop, nearly knocking over a vase. Like lightning, Harry moved to get it, catching the vase just before it fell to the floor. It was an incredible move—faster than humanly possible.

Harry looked up at Peter, surprise on his face. "Did you see that?"

I saw it, Peter thought, fighting back a wince. Harry might not remember the New Goblin, but he could still move like him. *I just hope his memory stays blank.* Peter forced a smile. "Guess you still got the moves," he said to his best friend.

Let's just hope you don't decide to use them.

Don't let one critic get you down, Mary Jane told herself as she walked into the theater. She stood straight, forcing herself to walk proudly. She didn't want the rest of the cast to know that she was upset by the review. *I can't let it affect my performance tonight*, she decided. *Peter's right. Those critics are thieves. They steal our potential.*

She pushed open the heavy lobby door and was surprised to hear someone singing her song. Looking up, she saw an actress onstage going through Mary Jane's dance moves for the opening number. It was someone Mary Jane had never seen before. When the actress caught sight of Mary Jane, she stopped singing. The rest of the cast had been watching from the audience and the wings, but when the music stopped, everyone turned to look at Mary Jane.

For a moment, nobody spoke.

The director turned to his assistant. "Didn't anybody call her?" he whispered.

Mary Jane's heart stopped. They had replaced her. One lousy review and they had already replaced her! "One critic?" she asked, tears welling in her eyes.

The play's producer eyed her coldly. "*All* the papers," he corrected.

This was news to Mary Jane. *All?* The lump in her throat was so large that she could hardly breathe. *Every critic in the city thought I was terrible?*

"If you'd like, we can say you became ill," the producer suggested.

Mary Jane didn't even reply. Her face burning, she turned and scurried out of the theater. She couldn't face them for a single moment longer.

Peter spotted Mary Jane in the crowd that had gathered to see Spider-Man. He immediately worked his way to her side. This was a very special day for Peter—Spider-Man was supposed to receive the key to the city. Peter thought about all of the nasty articles and editorials J.J. Jameson had printed about Spider-Man in the *Daily Bugle.* For a while, the people of New York seemed to think that Spider-Man was actually a menace to the city. But over the years, he had saved many lives. Now almost everyone recognized Spider-Man for the hero he was—everyone except J.J. Jameson.

Peter grinned at Mary Jane, the anticipation gathering in his chest. He was so excited about receiving the key to the city that he didn't even think to ask Mary Jane why she wasn't at the theater getting ready for her show.

Mary Jane looked at his eager face. She wanted to tell him what had just happened at the theater—how she had been humiliated in front of the entire cast. But this was *his* moment. She didn't have the heart to ruin it by confessing she'd just been fired. "I'm proud of you," she told Peter, and she meant it.

Peter pointed to a tall building at the corner of the square. "I'm planning to swing in from over there."

Mary Jane nodded. "Give them a good show," she said.

"You, too," Peter said with a smile. "Knock 'em dead tonight. And don't worry about that review— we'll laugh about it tomorrow." He hurried off to do his thing as Spider-Man.

"Yeah," Mary Jane whispered. But she knew that she wouldn't be laughing about that review. Not tomorrow—not ever.

Her career was over before it had even begun.

Nearby, Flint Marko scratched at his ear. It had been itching all day. *No wonder it's been bothering me,* he thought as a few grains of sand fell out. He tilted his head and knocked on the side of his skull. A stream of sand poured from his ear, blanketing the pavement at his feet.

That's better.

Just then, he noticed two police officers watching him. Flint could tell they recognized him. He ducked behind an empty truck and disappeared from sight as they hustled toward him.

I've got to hide, Flint thought. Luckily, he had the perfect solution—he could make himself into sand and hide in the back of the truck. Presto . . . the perfect disguise.

The police looked under the truck. They looked in the cab. Finally, one of them climbed on top of the truck. It was covered with a tarp. Suspicious, the officer yanked off the tarp . . . but all he found was a pile of sand.

It didn't make sense. That guy couldn't have just disappeared. The police officer picked up a shovel to investigate. . . .

Slam!

A gritty hand shot out of the sand and launched the cop into the air. He fell against a car as Flint Marko—now Sandman—rose out of the truck. Too shocked to cry out, the other officer opened fire. The bullets tore holes in the sand, sending particles flying. But Sandman kept on walking. Bullets couldn't stop him.

With all of the fury of a desert storm, Sandman blasted down the street.

In the square, the mayor's microphone gave a shriek of feedback as he began his speech. The raucous crowd shouted for Spider-Man, but the mayor ignored them, droning on and on despite the whistles, cheers, and boos.

Will this speech ever end? Mary Jane wondered

as she watched from the crowd. She was squeezed on either side—it looked like hundreds, maybe thousands—of people had turned out to watch Spider-Man get his key to the city.

Suddenly, a cheerful voice sounded behind her. "Hey, M.J.!"

Turning, Mary Jane found herself face-to-face with Harry Osborn. His eyes were gleaming as he flashed her a brilliant grin. Despite his fall, Harry looked healthy. He had only a small scrape on his forehead and he seemed happier than she had seen him in months. M.J. didn't know all the details of what had happened, only that Harry had been hurt.

"Where's Pete?" Harry asked, smiling as he looked around.

Mary Jane couldn't help smiling back. "Taking somebody's picture, I guess," she said with a shrug. It used to be that only two people knew that Peter was Spider-Man—Mary Jane and Harry. But when Peter and Mary Jane went to visit Harry in the hospital, they realized that Harry had lost his memory. So now only Mary Jane knew Peter's secret—and she was going to keep it that way.

Harry asked why Mary Jane was at the ceremony instead of the theater. Looking into his smiling face, Mary Jane felt like she could talk about it a little. She explained that she had been fired from her job, and Harry said that he was sorry.

"You look so good, Harry," Mary Jane said after a moment.

Harry shrugged and grinned. "It's a very strange feeling, not knowing exactly who you are." He knocked himself on the side of the head with the heel of his hand. "A bump on the head, and I'm free as a bird."

"Bump me on the head, will you?" Mary Jane joked.

He gave her a playful tap and Mary Jane laughed.

For the first time that afternoon, she wasn't thinking about the fact that she had just lost her job. Harry's good spirits were actually cheering her up.

Harry was just what she needed.

CHAPTER 5

Gwen Stacy looked nervously out at the crowd as she smoothed the front of her blouse. True, she was a model, but she had never spoken in front of so many people before. Her heart was pounding in her ears, and it wasn't just the crowd that was making her uneasy.

Gwen was nervous because she knew that *he* was out there. Somewhere close by, Spider-Man was listening to the speeches and cheers. And he would be here any moment—in person—to accept the key to the city.

Stepping up to the podium, Gwen leaned toward the microphone. "I'm here today," she said as slowly and distinctly as she could, "speaking to you only because I fell sixty-two stories out of a building . . . and someone caught me."

The crowd went wild. A cheer like a tidal wave rose from them, breaking over Gwen, nearly drowning her in noise. She peered toward the buildings. No sign of him yet. But he was on his way.

She was sure of it.

Nearby, Spider-Man crouched on the side of a building, listening to the New York City crowd go wild. Below him, people were packed into the square. He smiled to himself. "They love me," he whispered.

I guess this is how it feels to be a hero, Spider-Man thought. It was funny: When he was busy saving people or stopping crime, he never felt very heroic. But right now, clinging to the side of a wall, he felt important.

He felt like the city appreciated him.

A marching band struck up a cheerful rendition

of the hero's theme as Spider-Man swung over the crowd. The whistles and cheers were deafening as he lowered himself toward Gwen. Once he was face-to-face with her, he paused, still upside down.

Gwen didn't know what made her do it, but when she saw Spider-Man so close, she reached out and pulled up his mask. Not all the way—just enough to reveal his mouth.

I just want to thank him for saving me, Gwen thought. But in her heart, she knew that it was more than that. Spider-Man was amazing. He was brave. He was unique.

Gwen passed Spider-Man the key. But before he could thank her, Gwen pressed her lips against his.

The crowd hooted and hollered, encouraging Gwen as the kiss went on.

Only one person in the crowd wasn't cheering. Mary Jane watched the scene onstage, horrified. It was exactly how she had first kissed Spider-Man—she stood on the ground, her head tilted up toward his. It had been raining that night, and Mary Jane could almost feel the drops on her skin as she watched the scene play again before her.

That's us, she thought as she watched Spider-Man kiss Gwen Stacy. *Only that isn't* me *he's kissing!*

Tears welled in her eyes and she turned away. Suddenly, all of the horrible feelings that had threatened to overwhelm her earlier returned.

It was more than Mary Jane could take.

This time, not even Harry would be able to cheer her up.

Meanwhile, a storm was gathering near the excited crowd. A sixty-foot sandstorm, to be exact. The cloud of sand thundered around a corner and suddenly—like a puff of smoke—vanished into thin air. The crowd scattered in all directions, trying to escape the harsh winds. Spider-Man's Spidey sense tingled.

Then, like a tornado descending from the sky, a sand cloud swirled madly around an armored car. The heavy metal truck nearly disappeared in the violent whirlwind. The armored vehicle was transporting money from a bank to a depository, and was full of cash and gold. The truck weighed more than a ton, but it shook like a leaf in a thunderstorm. The sand easily tore the top off of the armored car and descended upon the city.

Sandman had arrived.

From the front cab, one of the brown-uniformed guards turned and shot a blast at Sandman, who had just appeared behind them, blowing away part of the villain's face. Sandman let out a cry—howling in pain—and in the next moment, he dissolved. A wave of sand smashed from the rear of the armored car, swooping forward to engulf both the guard and the driver behind the wheel.

Desperate and running out of air, the driver pressed his foot against the accelerator pedal. The armored car started to move forward! It barreled down the street at top speed.

Thump.

The metal floor of the armed car made only the slightest noise as Spider-Man dropped inside and stood beside Sandman. He was human-sized now, and looked very much like a sandy version of his old self, Flint Marko, as he bent over to gather sacks of cash and gold coins.

"Don't you know there's a penalty for early withdrawal?" Spider-Man quipped.

Looking up, Sandman glared at Spider-Man. "Back off," Flint warned. He wasn't joking. He needed that money, and he would do anything to get it. He wasn't about to let anyone—including Spider-Man—stop him.

Spider-Man didn't back down. But neither did Sandman. The two stood there, facing off in the back of the moving truck. But Flint wasn't afraid of a hero with super spider-powers. *I have super sand-powers,* he thought. *We'll have to see whose powers are stronger.*

Sure enough, Spider-Man struck, launching his fist at Flint. Sandman shifted slightly, and Spider-Man's hand went right through Sandman's body . . . and came out on the other side.

Flint gathered the mass of his sand and slammed Spider-Man with a hammer fist. The blow was like being hit with a huge brick. It blasted Spider-Man against the back of the truck. The door ripped away from its hinges and it, Sandman, and Spider-Man spun sprawling into the street that zipped past below them.

Sandman rolled away, disappearing in a swirl of sand, but Spider-Man landed on his feet on top of the metal door. He shot over the smooth asphalt street like a surfer. Sparks flew from the door as it trailed behind the truck. Thinking fast, Spider-Man slung a web at the back of the armored car. He rode the door like a wakeboard.

Honk!

Spider-Man dodged suddenly as he almost collided with an oncoming car. The traffic was thick, and he had to weave between vehicles to avoid being crushed.

Meanwhile, the armored car sped forward.

This can't go on forever! Spider-Man thought. *I have to stop that truck before it runs into something!* The guards were still unconscious in the front seat. If the truck hit something, they would be killed.

Hand over hand, he managed to pull himself back toward the guards.

The truck was out of control—and headed right for a brick wall! Spider-Man knew that he had to do something fast to save the guards. With a lot of effort, Spider-Man yanked himself into the speeding car. He spun a web around the unconscious guards, pulling them from the front of the truck and tossing them away from the vehicle. With a quick zap, Spider-Man made a net, and the two guards fell gently against it and hung there, safe. But the armored car was still moving at top speed and there was no time for Spider-Man to get out!

In the next moment, there was a crash of crunching metal as the armored car smashed into a brick wall. The noise was deafening for one brutal moment, and then everything went completely, suddenly silent. There was no movement except for the steam that rose from the hissing engine.

Finally, Spider-Man managed to collect himself. Pain tore through his shoulder and legs as he crawled from the wreckage. It was a miracle that he wasn't seriously hurt. A crash like that would have killed almost anyone.

But, of course, Spider-Man wasn't just anyone.

Still, he had been beaten by Sandman. *This isn't good*, Spider-Man thought. Not good at all. He'd been clobbered . . . right after receiving the key to the city!

Spider-Man shook the sand from his body. *Ugh*, he thought, as he yanked off a boot and turned it upside down.

A pile of sand spilled onto the street.

Spider-Man shook his head. "Where do these guys come from?"

The next day, the *Daily Bugle* ran a front-page photograph of Sandman with letters three inches tall: SANDMAN! proclaimed the headline. SON OF A BEACH! EVEN SPIDER-MAN CAN'T STOP HIM!

Below was a note from the editor-in-chief. BUGLE CALL: GIVE BACK THE KEY!

Peter shook his head and slapped the paper on his kitchen table. *Give back the key*, he thought solemnly as he pulled on his best shirt. *How can they say that? It's not like I didn't try to stop that crazy sand guy!*

The paper barely even mentioned that Spider-Man had saved the guards. They spent most of the space in the article using words like "invincible," "indestructible," and "dangerous." The whole thing was about Sandman, of course.

Worst of all, the story came with a photo, courtesy of Eddie Brock.

Don't think about it, Peter told himself. After all, this was his big night. He couldn't think about Sandman right now—he had more important things on his mind.

Things like Mary Jane.

Ignoring the ache in his shoulder, Peter yanked on his jacket. He grabbed part of a stack of money from his drawer . . . then took the rest. He was going to need every dime tonight. *Hey,* he thought, his heart pounding excitedly in his chest, *what's money for? It's for spending on a special occasion, right?*

Reaching into his pocket, Peter pulled out Aunt May's diamond engagement ring. Still there. Still safe.

Suddenly, his Spidey sense started to tingle. *What's that?* he thought, turning. But he didn't see anything.

I'm just nervous, Peter told himself. *It's making me jumpy. It's natural to feel nervous before you ask the girl of your dreams to marry you.*

Taking a deep breath, Peter put the ring back in his pocket and headed out the door. He didn't look back. . . .

Which is why he didn't see the black goo oozing its way along the wall of his apartment and toward his closet.

CHAPTER 6

Whoa, Peter thought as he walked through the front entrance to the Constellation Restaurant. It was the most elegant place he had ever seen. Crystal chandeliers glittered like diamonds from the high ceilings. Candlelight sent a rosy glow over snowy tablecloths at each table. The delicate clink of expensive glasses floated through the air as the beautifully dressed men and women at each table chatted and laughed over plates of elegant food. Peter caught the scent of something delicious as he walked up to the maître d's table. Peter was wearing his best clothes, but he felt underdressed and out of place. Still, this restaurant was definitely special. He knew that Mary Jane would love it.

The maître d' gave Peter a look. "Bonsoir," he said in perfect, clipped French. Then he said something else in French—Peter had no idea what. *He's probably asking if I have a reservation,* he reasoned.

Peter gave the maître d' his name. "I have a request," he said, once his name had been found on the list. He cleared his throat. "I have this . . . ring . . ." He held up Aunt May's little diamond. ". . . and, uh . . ."

At the sight of the ring, the maître d's black eyebrows lifted and his lips curled into a smile. "You will pop the question tonight?" he asked in a heavy French accent. A moment ago, he had been reserved, even haughty, but the idea of romance brought out a gleam of excitement in the Frenchman's eyes. "Maybe you will put the ring in the bottom of her glass?" he suggested.

Peter nodded. That was just what he had

Spider-Man is on
top of the world.

Peter and Mary Jane visit Harry at the hospital.

Peter gets his best friend back.

In a flash, Flint Marko is forever changed.

There's a new villain in town: Sandman.

A mysterious black goo creeps over Spider-Man.

Spider-Man sees his new reflection.

... he sheds his black suit.

Eddie discovers Peter's secret.

Will Spider-Man escape
from Venom's evil grip?

The new Peter shows
Eddie Brock who's boss.

The new suit sits in Peter's closet . . .
waiting for him.

Spider-Man knows
what must be done . . .

been thinking—he'd give Mary Jane a glass of champagne with the ring in it. Peter had been a little worried that maybe Mary Jane would accidentally swallow the ring, so he was glad that the maître d'—who clearly had experience with this stuff—thought it was a good idea, too. "Also," Peter said as he held out a slip of paper, "I thought at the same time, if the violins could play this song. . . ."

The maître d' glanced at the paper and nodded approvingly. "Their favorite," he said with a blissful sigh.

"Take good care of the ring," Peter said nervously as he handed it over.

The maître d' smiled reassuringly as he led Peter to his table.

As he sat alone, waiting for Mary Jane to arrive, Peter shifted in his chair. "Would you like some champagne?" he asked in a low voice, rehearsing. "Oh. How'd that get in there?" His blue eyes widened in mock surprise as he gazed at the invisible glass in Mary Jane's hand. "Oh, stop. Don't cry."

At that moment, Mary Jane appeared at the entrance to the restaurant. Peter gave her a small wave as she shuffled toward him, looking morose. Mary Jane had just taken a new job—as a singing waitress in a jazz club. The place was slightly seedy, and she'd have to work late shifts. It was a long way down from a spot on Broadway, but she needed the money. She glanced around the glamorous restaurant with barely a spark of interest. "This place in your budget?" she asked as she slid into the seat opposite Peter's.

"It's a special occasion," Peter replied brightly. He gave Mary Jane a broad smile. "You're on Broadway. You're a star."

Mary Jane looked down at the tablecloth. She opened her mouth to tell Peter the truth—that she wasn't on Broadway anymore—but she couldn't make the words come out. She didn't want to talk about it. It was too painful. "I don't feel like much of a star tonight," she admitted instead.

"You are a star, and you've earned it." Peter's voice was warm. He could tell that Mary Jane was down. *Probably still worrying about that review*, he thought. But he wasn't about to let that critic spoil this special night. *After all, this is the moment we'll remember for the rest of our lives,* he reasoned, *not one bad review.*

Peter was about to say more, but at that moment Gwen—who had been having dinner with her parents at a nearby table—stopped by to say hello. With a gracious smile, she introduced herself to Mary Jane. "It's so nice to meet you," Gwen said. "Pete talks about you all the time."

Mary Jane lifted her eyebrows at Peter. She recognized Gwen from Spider-Man's key-to-the-city ceremony. Mary Jane hadn't realized that the pretty girl Spider-Man had been kissing onstage was actually someone Peter knew. The image of their kiss had seared itself into her memory.

Peter cleared his throat. "Gwen's my, uh, lab partner," he stuttered, "in Dr. Connors's class." He blushed under Mary Jane's intense stare.

"Peter saved my life in chemistry." Gwen said with a laugh. Then she asked Peter if he had a photo of Spider-Man kissing her at the ceremony. It was something she'd love to have as a memento, she explained. But deep down, Gwen knew that it was more than that. She still got a little thrill every time she thought about sweeping through the air in his arms . . . and the kiss they shared at the center of the city. "Who gets kissed by Spider-Man these days?" she asked Mary Jane with a playful laugh.

"I can't imagine," Mary Jane said dryly, giving Peter an angry glare.

Gwen looked from Mary Jane back to Peter. "I'll leave you two alone," she said, sensing the awkwardness. She gave a small wave and crossed back to her table.

Peter waved after her. Distracted by Mary Jane's anger, he didn't notice that across the room the maître d' was nodding at his wave. Thinking it was the signal that Peter was about to propose, he scurried off to bring the champagne.

Mary Jane leaned back in her chair and studied Peter's face. "Let me ask you something," she said slowly. She looked over at Gwen. "When you kissed her . . . who was kissing her? Spider-Man?" Mary Jane's eyes clicked on Peter's, making him squirm. "Or Peter?"

"What do you mean?" Peter asked. His hand played with the silverware on the table.

"That was *our* kiss." There was a slight quaver in Mary Jane's voice. She couldn't help it. The image of Peter kissing someone else in front of all of those people . . . it was too much. "Why would you do that?" her voice was almost a whisper.

"She's a girl in my class, Mary Jane," Peter said. He was trying to sound reasonable, but the truth was, he wasn't sure how to answer the question. He wasn't sure why he had kissed Gwen. He was just swept up in the moment. All of the people were cheering, and Spider-Man was finally getting some respect—

"I guess I thought you were going to . . ." Mary Jane swallowed hard. *He isn't going to apologize,* she realized. *He isn't going to say that he's sorry that he hurt my feelings!* She remembered the other day when she had needed him to stay with her, to console her about her lousy review. He hadn't done that, either. Then she had been fired, and Peter didn't even know. Now she had a crummy new job, and she didn't feel like she could tell him about it. *What's happening to us?* she wondered, feeling miserable. "It doesn't matter," Mary Jane said quickly. "I don't feel very well. I have to go." She stood up, but her knees felt weak as she hurried toward the exit.

At that moment, a violinist approached the table. He was playing the song Peter had requested: "Falling in Love."

But Mary Jane's back was to the table. She never saw the violinist. She was already out the door.

Not realizing that Peter had been deserted, the maître d' walked up to him with two glasses of champagne on a silver tray.

Glumly, Peter took the one with the ring at the bottom and fished it out.

Well, Aunt May told me to make the proposal memorable, he thought miserably. *I guess it was, because I have a feeling I'll remember this moment for the rest of my life.*

Peter stood at the pay phone in the hallway outside of his apartment. It was the only phone he had. Peter had just left Mary Jane a message on her answering machine, begging her to call him. He couldn't believe that he had botched the proposal so badly. *I really should have apologized about the whole Gwen thing*, he thought. *That was dumb. I shouldn't have let a silly argument set this night out of control.*

How did this night go so wrong? Peter wondered, his fingers still wrapped around the black plastic receiver. It buzzed in his hand as the phone rang.

Expecting Mary Jane, Peter yanked it off of the cradle right away. But it was a man's voice at the other end of the line.

"Mr. Parker," the voice said, "this is Detective Neil Garrett, from the thirty-second precinct. I'm calling on behalf of Captain Stacy. We've got some new information regarding the homicide of your uncle, Ben Parker."

New information? Peter wondered. But Uncle Ben's killer was caught long ago. *What kind of information could they have? Why were they still investigating the case?* It was closed long ago. Peter asked a few questions, but Detective Garrett didn't want to go into the details over the phone.

Peter told him that he would come down to the station house right away.

Aunt May sat as still as a stone in the chair beside Peter's. Across the desk was the large form of Captain Stacy. The captain looked tired—as though he'd had a long day of telling people news they didn't want to hear. Still, Peter could see the resemblance between the police captain and his daughter, Gwen. They had the same eyes, and Captain Stacy's were edged with concern as he began to explain why he had brought Aunt May and Peter down to the station.

"Originally, we thought that this man, Dennis Caradine, was your husband's killer," Captain Stacy said to Aunt May as he held up a picture. The face was as familiar to Peter as his own. It was the man he had seen running away from Uncle Ben after the murder. Captain Stacy placed the photo on his desk. "We were wrong."

Peter's heart froze in his chest. *Wrong? How could that be?*

Aunt May looked shocked. "What?"

"The actual killer is still at large," the captain explained, holding up another photo. "He's a small-time crook who has been in and out of prison." Peter gaped at the picture in Captain Stacy's hand. The man was a stranger to him. "Two days ago, he escaped," the captain went on. "Evidently, he confessed his guilt to a cellmate. And we have two witnesses."

Peter felt as though he wasn't getting enough oxygen—he couldn't breathe. *Uncle Ben had been killed by someone else. Someone else . . . this stranger.* It was taking a moment for his brain to process what that meant. That meant that Dennis Caradine had died . . . for nothing. . . . ?

"I watched my uncle die." Peter's voice was trembling with rage. "And we went after the wrong man. And now you're saying you had suspicions for *two years*?" His voice was rising—it was all he could do to keep from screaming. Why hadn't anyone let him know? *If I had known that he may not have been guilty, Spider-Man never would have*— But he couldn't even finish the thought. It was too horrible. "This man killed my uncle," Peter shouted, "and he's still out there!"

It was too much. Too much.

Peter stormed out of the precinct. He had to get out of there. He couldn't bear to look at Captain Stacy—or think about Dennis Caradine—for another moment.

CHAPTER 7

A gust of sand howled through the streets, hurling itself against buildings and flinging itself through alleys. People closed their eyes and turned away as sand bit at their faces, tearing at their clothes. The storm moved furiously, never stopping, never slowing until it reached its destination—a medical research facility, where a doctor in a white lab coat sat, blinking at what was left of his research.

Dr. Wallace had worked tirelessly for years, trying to find a cure for a rare disease. But the sickness was challenging, and even though he'd had a team of excellent doctors and scientists working with him for a long time, they hadn't managed to make much progress. Now it looked as though his research had hit a dead end. He had lost most of his funding. People didn't believe that he would ever find a cure.

"Hello?" Dr. Wallace called as the overhead lights dimmed, flickered, and went out. In another moment, the generators kicked in, and the lab was awash in dim emergency lighting. For a moment, the doctor thought that the vision before him was the result of bad light. It was grainy and indistinct, but almost human. "Who are you?"

Flint Marko stepped out of the shadows. "It's me," he said in his gravelly voice. "Flint Marko."

Dr. Wallace searched his memory. He couldn't remember ever meeting a Flint Marko, although the name was familiar. But, certainly, he couldn't forget meeting someone like this. . . .

"I wrote you from prison," Flint explained, "about my daughter, Penny. She still needs your help."

Dr. Wallace sighed. *Penny Marko.* Yes, he remembered her. She was a sweet, gravely ill little girl. This was the part of his job that Dr. Wallace despised the most—telling parents that their children would not recover. It never got easier. "I didn't have the funding to finish the research," the doctor began to explain.

Flint Marko pulled out a sack of cash—one of the many he had stolen from the armored car. "Well," he said with a slow smile, "try this."

Dr. Wallace blinked at the money in surprise. It was clearly a vast sum. Still, it wasn't enough. "It would take teams of researchers," he said, shaking his head, "and millions of dollars."

"Then I'll get more!" Flint shouted.

The doctor tried to keep his voice even. He knew that Flint Marko was a dangerous man, and he didn't want to upset him. But he couldn't lie, either. False hope was a dangerous thing, the doctor knew. "Even if you could," the doctor explained, "it's highly unlikely we'd find a cure in the short time your daughter has left—"

"Shut up!" Wind howled through the lab as

Flint slammed the doctor through a window between offices. Glass showered down on him as the doctor hit the floor. "Just find a cure for my Penny!" Flint snarled.

The doctor held up his hands. "I will! Don't hurt me!"

Flint brought his face up close to the doctor's. He didn't want to hurt the doctor—but he would do what he had to do to save his daughter. "Then don't fail me," he growled.

The doctor nodded. He would do his best to save Flint Marko's daughter. He didn't know if it was possible, but he knew he had to try.

Now two lives were counting on it.

Peter could hardly bear to stand up when he heard the gentle knock at the door. His emotions were weighing him down—first the fight with Mary Jane, then the news about his uncle. Wearily, he peered through the peephole. It was Mary Jane—the one person who could get him to open the door.

Still, he was too upset about Uncle Ben's killer

to feel happy to see her. His plan to ask her to marry him seemed far away now, like a dream. He didn't know what to say. Luckily, Mary Jane did the talking for him.

"Aunt May called me," Mary Jane said to Peter. "She told me about this convict and what he did to Uncle Ben. She's worried about you."

Peter didn't speak as he turned and retreated into his apartment. Mary Jane followed, closing the door behind her.

Her heart ached for Peter. It had been a difficult few days for her, but she couldn't imagine going through what Peter had to face right now. "You hunted down the wrong man," she said, "but you couldn't have known when you pushed him that he wasn't—"

"He had a gun on me," Peter snapped. Anger wormed its way through his voice. "I made a move. He fell. I didn't push him." Still, Peter felt sick. He had thought that Dennis Caradine's death was a sort of justice. And even if Caradine was an accomplice in the robbery, it still wasn't just. Not at all.

"I'm not accusing you of anything," Mary Jane

said quickly, regretting the words she had chosen. She had been trying to help, not to make things worse. "If I can help you in some way, I'm here to . . ." *Oh, why am I here?* she thought suddenly. *What on earth do I think I can do to help?* She didn't have an answer. All she knew was that if she were in Peter's situation, she would want *him* to be there for *her.* ". . . to be here . . ." she finished lamely. "I just want—"

"Thank you for coming." Peter's voice was flat, lifeless. He held open the door for Mary Jane, signaling that she should go. Peter really wished that he had the energy to talk to Mary Jane, but what he needed was to be alone. He had to think. He had to think about how he could make things right.

Mary Jane paused at the door. "We all need help sometimes, Peter," she said.

Help? Peter thought. *Nobody can help me.*

Peter didn't say good-bye as she walked out.

Once she was gone, Peter turned up the volume on his police scanner. *This guy is out there,* he thought. *Countless other crooks are out there, too. Crime might be down, but the city is still crawling with criminals.* Peter thought about Sandman, and how he had beaten Spider-Man in a fight. *That's not going to happen again,* Peter vowed. *Anyone who tries to hurt someone in this city is going to have to face me.*

Criminals may escape the cops, and they may escape justice, but they can't escape Spider-Man.

Darkness fell outside Peter's window, turning the sky an inky black. In the corner, the police scanner droned on. "Car 604, domestic disturbance, 3415 Belmont, Apartment B, woman caller is being held at knife-point. . . ."

Peter's eyes moved back and forth beneath his lids. He was in his spider suit, but he was fast asleep. He was in the deepest part of his dream as the black goo oozed from his closet and moved toward his bed.

Peter moaned as his dreams turned dark. He was having a nightmare—Dennis Caradine was falling, falling, falling to his death. Over and over,

Peter saw the same image as the slippery goo spread over him, turning his dreams darker, his anger hotter, and seeping thickly into his red-and-blue suit. . . .

When Peter woke up, he found himself looking down at the city below. Traffic and people as small as ants rushed across the pavement under his head. Looking up, he realized that he was suspended from a thread at one of the highest points in New York City. *What's going on?* Peter wondered. *What happened?* Just then, he caught sight of himself in an office window. His spider suit—it was *black*!

"Whoa!"

Admiring himself, Peter leaped to the side of the mirrored building and clung there. His muscles felt taut, strong. Peter flexed his arm—there was no doubt about it, his muscles had grown overnight. He felt amazing! His whole body was tingling, and Peter was itching *to move*.

Faster than he ever thought possible, Peter ran straight down the side of the building. With

an enormous leap, he vaulted into a midair som-
ersault, then landed on a narrow ledge. It was an
impossible jump—one he never would have tried
the day before. But with this new black suit, he
felt like he could do anything.

I don't know what happened to you, suit, Peter
thought as he checked out his new look. *All I
know is that I like it.*

CHAPTER 8

Spider-Man slithered across the jet-black ceiling. He was deep in the belly of the city, crawling through the maze of tunnels that formed New York's subway system. He was hunting. Hunting for justice. *Criminals are out there*, Spider-Man thought as he crept forward in the dark, *and every single one of them is going to have to deal with me.*

He wasn't going to wait anymore. His new black suit made him want to go out and *do* something. So when Peter had heard something over the police scanner about a disturbance on the subway's "money train," he sprang into action. He knew that it had to be Sandman. Who else would be bold enough to take on one of the best-defended trains in the country? *He's not going to get away this time*, Spider-Man decided. Warm anger rose in his throat as he remembered how Sandman had practically killed him. It was time to show the city that Spider-Man was still willing and able to take on anybody. *The crooks need to know that they aren't running this city*, he thought.

A train horn sounded and Spider-Man flattened himself at the highest point in the curve of the ceiling. The train swooshed by just below him, sending a gust of wind down the length of his body.

Once the train had passed, Spider-Man moved on. As he turned around the corner, he found what he was looking for. Sure enough, Sandman appeared—a grainy monster holding sacks of cash.

Spider-Man made a slight movement, just enough to send a sound echoing through the tunnel. At the noise, Sandman spun around to face him, unleashing a roar.

But Spider-Man was gone. He had disappeared into the darkness of the subway. Sandman squinted against the black, trying to see. But the new black suit hid Spider-Man, making him almost invisible.

Slam!

Spider-Man smashed Sandman in the face with a brutal blow. Sandman staggered backward, and the sacks of money dropped from his hands.

"What do you want?" he roared.

Justice, Spider-Man thought. Rage pulsed through his body, heating his skin like an electric blanket. His muscles twitched under the power of the Black Suit. *I want the justice that Uncle Ben deserved, but never got. And I'm going to get that justice—I'll never stop until I get it. And you're the first on my list.*

But that isn't what he said.

He dropped to the floor so that he was face-to-face with the villain. "I'm gonna beat you up real bad," Spider-Man said to Sandman. "And then I'm going to do it again. And then I'm going to take what's left of you back to prison." It wasn't the kind of thing Spider-Man usually said, or even felt. But Spider-Man was angry and the suit made him feel like he could say and do anything.

Sandman shook his head. "That ain't going to happen," he snarled, planting his feet wide. An image of his sick little girl popped into his mind. Sandman wasn't about to let Spider-Man stop him from saving Penny—he didn't care what color his suit was. "I've got an important thing to take care of."

"I will never step aside for you," Spider-Man spat. He held up his hands and signaled to Sandman to hit him with his best shot. "Bring it."

A train horn blew as Sandman charged at Spider-Man, lowering his head for full impact. He clobbered Spider-Man, and the two sprawled across a web of tracks—they were at the intersection of several train lines. Spider-Man moved quickly to avoid being crushed as a train whooshed by.

Honk!

Another train pounded toward him at full speed. *Slam!* Sandman hit him with his fist, but Spider-Man blasted back. The two rolled over as another train rushed by, missing them by inches. In the next moment, Spider-Man felt hot air whip past him as another train rushed in the opposite direction.

Slam!

Sandman knocked Spider-Man backward, catching his heel on a piece of track. Spider-Man fired a web as they both fell across the rails.

Sandman grinned. The web had missed him by a mile! He lunged forward to strike. . . .

But in the next moment, he noticed that Spider-Man didn't seem concerned. When he turned to look, Sandman saw that the web had hit a train switch. With a grinding metallic click, the tracks shifted, meeting in a new place—directly beneath Sandman's hands.

Honk!

A train plowed forward—directly over Sandman's wrists. Sand poured from the stumps at the ends of his arms, creating a giant dune. With an ugly scream, Sandman lunged forward, burying Spider-Man in a huge dune. Spider-Man struggled for breath, but the sand continued to stream from Sandman's body, the pile growing larger and larger until it pulled Spider-Man under.

A long moment passed, and then Spider-Man's black hand appeared. He shot a web toward the ceiling and caught a pipe. With a mighty yank, the pipe gave way, dousing both him and the pile of sand around him with a fierce stream of water.

Sandman gave a hideous cry as water poured over him, turning him to mud and muck. The water swirled and rolled, washing the enormous sandpile down a subway drain.

Spider-Man looked down at the drain. Sandman had dissolved. All that was left of him was a tiny clump of sandy mud.

And Spider-Man didn't feel bad about it. Not even a little bit.

🕷 🕷 🕷

"Rent!" Peter's landlord shouted as Peter walked into his building later that day.

Nearby, the landlord's sweet but painfully shy daughter cowered as her father bellowed like an angry bull.

Peter's landlord was always shouting about the rent. That was because Peter was always late in paying it. Peter tried as hard as he could, but it wasn't easy to pay for the overpriced apartment. He didn't make much money as a freelance photographer, and it was hard to earn more when he spent so much of his time "volunteering" as Spider-Man.

"Rent!" cried the landlord, but this time, Peter couldn't take it anymore.

"Maybe I would consider paying the rent if you fixed *anything* in the building. Like the door! The broken door to my apartment, which is—at this very moment—unlocked!" he shouted furiously.

Without thinking, Peter grabbed the door. The anger and the black suit beneath his clothes made him incredibly strong, and the landlord could only gape as Peter ripped it off of its hinges.

Peter slammed into his apartment, enraged. But as he walked past a mirror, something caught his eye and made him pause. Stopping, he looked himself full in the face. He barely recognized what he saw.

Peter's blue eyes were huge, his teeth bared like a wild animal. His face was contorted in rage, and he looked vicious, crazed—even dangerous.

It's the suit, Peter realized. He was wearing it under his clothes, and he could still feel the pressure of the black fabric on his skin. *It's affecting me. It's making me stronger, sure, but I feel . . . different.*

The thought sent a shudder through him. He knew what he had to do. He couldn't wear the suit anymore—no matter how strong it made him. A Spider-Man who was out of control and unpredictable could do far more harm than good—like what he did to Sandman that afternoon. Before, he would have tried his hardest to bring a criminal to justice. Spider-Man caught criminals—it was the courts' job to punish them. But today, he had taken the punishment into his own hands. He didn't regret it, but he didn't want to do it again.

I should get rid of the suit. But he couldn't just throw it in a Dumpster. What if someone found it?

I should destroy it! he thought, but he didn't like that idea either.

Peter's sight landed on a trunk in the corner of the room. He took off his clothes, removed the suit, and put it in the trunk.

I'll keep it, he thought. *I just won't wear it. Ever again.*

Harry Osborn was humming to himself as he painted. He had forgotten how much he enjoyed putting brush to canvas, swirling colors across the blank white and making an image take shape.

Ever since his accident, Harry had been doing all sorts of artistic things, like writing poetry, reading, singing, and drawing. He also spent a lot of time outdoors, exercising and enjoying his strong, quick body. But painting was his real passion. It was something he enjoyed almost as much as he enjoyed Mary Jane's company. She had called to tell him that she had found a new job as a waitress in a jazz club. It wasn't great, but it was something, and Harry suggested that they have lunch together to celebrate. Harry glanced around the room and his eyes met his reflection in the full-length mirror on the wall—

Harry gasped as a sudden vision popped into his mind: the sight of his father's limp body. Spider-Man had killed him. . . .

Harry held his head. Where had this vision come from?

"You've taken your eye off the ball," said the voice of Norman Osborn—from inside his head. He appeared in the mirror, frowning at his son. He glanced quickly at the canvas in front of Harry, scowling at it in disgust.

Harry gaped at the mirror. He lifted his hand, reached out, stretched his fingertips toward the image of his father. . . .

Flash!

Memories poured into Harry's mind like water from a tap. His father's death, Spider-Man lying on the chaise longue, a hand removing

Spider-Man's mask, Peter at the theater, Mary Jane and Peter, the midair battle with Spider-Man, everything. . . .

"Where've you been?" Norman asked from his place in the mirror. He sneered at his son. "Remember me?"

"Yes, father." Harry's voice was quiet. He didn't feel like himself. He felt almost as though he was in a dream. "I remember everything."

"You haven't killed Peter Parker," Harry's father scolded.

This snapped Harry out of his trance. *Kill Peter?* But Peter was his best friend! No matter what, they were friends.

"I won't listen to you anymore," Harry shouted. "Let me be!"

Peter stepped gingerly into Dr. Connors's office. He hated to disturb his professor, but this was important. The black goo had taken over his suit . . . and Peter was worried about it.

At first, the professor wasn't thrilled to be interrupted to look at a strange specimen. But something in Peter's face told Dr. Connors that it was important. Very important. Besides, the black goo seemed interesting.

Dr. Connors promised to get back to Peter as soon as he could.

Mary Jane arrived at Harry's apartment a short while later. With a warm smile, he led her into the kitchen and started to cook. He chopped up some vegetables with the speed and precision of a professional chef, and cracked a few eggs into a bowl. Then he poured the eggs into a pan and began cooking an omelet. He arranged the vegetables in a complex pattern of colors and textures, then playfully flipped the omelet in the pan. Mary Jane laughed. She felt wonderful.

When the omelet was finished, it was so pretty that Mary Jane almost hated to eat it. Almost. But the first bite was so delicious, she knew that she'd finish everything on her plate.

In fact, Mary Jane was feeling so much better that she managed to tell Harry about her new job as a singing waitress. It wasn't so bad, really. At least she got to sing.

Harry was very understanding. He wanted to cheer Mary Jane up, so as they were eating, Harry shyly admitted that he had written a play for Mary Jane ages ago, when they were both in high school. He had recently come across it when he was sorting through a few things.

Harry asked her whether she would like to take a look at it. Mary Jane agreed, and read part of it aloud.

"Harry," she said as she read the last line, "it's beautiful."

Harry smiled at her. "Would you like the part?"

"Thank you." Mary Jane's voice was grateful. After feeling so rejected by the Broadway theater, it was nice to know that someone still thought she was a good actress. *Harry has done so much to cheer me up*, she thought. *I don't know if he realizes how much it means to me. I just wish I could find a way to tell Peter about every-thing. . . .* "I'd love to be in your play." She sighed thoughtfully.

Warmth bloomed in Harry's chest as a memory

came flooding back. He had loved Mary Jane! *Yes, and I still love her,* Harry realized, leaning forward. He pressed his lips against hers.

Mary Jane pulled away, torn. It wasn't that she didn't love Harry—she did. As a friend. *But I could never love Harry the way I love Peter,* she thought.

Harry studied her face. Another memory had just surfaced. *That's right—she loves Peter. I'm jealous of my best friend.* "You're thinking about Peter, aren't you?"

Mary Jane winced. Harry looked strangely angry, and it made her feel awkward. "I guess I am," she admitted, adding that she had to go. She couldn't stay there with Harry—not after he'd tried to kiss her.

A feeling of rage rose in Harry's chest as Mary Jane rose to leave. *That's right,* he thought furiously, *go running to Peter—just like you always do!* The memories were tumbling in now, swirling like a hurricane. Peter—jealousy—Mary Jane—love—Peter—Spider-Man. . . . At last, the final piece fell into place. Harry could hear his father's voice laughing from the back of his mind.

If Mary Jane leaves me alone with my father, Harry thought, *he'll make me do something awful. He'll try to make me hurt Mary Jane and Peter—and I don't want to! They're my friends!*

But then another voice popped into his head. "No, they're not! Peter Parker is your enemy! Don't you remember? He has stolen everything you ever loved!

"Let her go!" the voice in his mind commanded.

"Don't leave me alone!" Harry begged, but Mary Jane was already out the door.

"There, there," Norman said with false kindness.

Harry put his hands to his head. His father had him.

He had him, and he knew it.

Peter Parker walked beneath the fresh green branches, holding a bouquet of his girlfriend's favorite flowers. There had been something in Mary Jane's voice when she called—something that made him think to buy the flowers. She had sounded weary and sad. She needed cheering up, that much was clear. *I've been thinking only*

about myself, Peter had thought. *I need to focus on Mary Jane.*

The sun shone through the halo of her red hair as she sat on the wooden park bench. Peter held out the flowers. "Peonies," he said.

Mary Jane's heart felt tight as she looked down at the beautiful pink flowers. Their light, sweet fragrance wafted toward her nose. *My favorite*, she thought, thrilled that Peter had remembered. But in a way, it only made things harder for her. She knew what she had to say to Peter—but she didn't want to say it. *But you have to*, she thought, clearing her throat. *Just get it over with.* "There's something I have to tell you, Pete," Mary Jane said as Peter settled onto the bench beside her. "This is not easy for me. But I have to be honest. We can't be together anymore."

Peter felt as though he had been stabbed—the pain was that quick, and that intense. *Can't be together? Mary Jane is breaking up with me?* "But I love you," he said, reaching for her hand.

Mary Jane looked at him sharply. She knew that he was telling the truth, even if he hadn't been able to show it lately. Even her jealousy over the fact that Spider-Man had kissed Gwen didn't seem important. Mary Jane knew that she was the only woman Peter had ever loved. Still, none of that mattered. "Love doesn't matter if you're lonely."

"That's crazy," Peter insisted. His mind was swimming.

How can I put an end to this? Mary Jane thought. She couldn't bear to sit here and argue with Peter. She didn't want to be saying this in the first place! *I have to give him an excuse that he can't fight. I have to give him something final.* "The truth is," Mary Jane said slowly, "there's someone else. There's no more to talk about."

Peter looked into Mary Jane's face. Her voice sounded certain, but something told him that he should fight to keep her. *A few days ago, I was about to propose. I want to marry this woman,* Peter thought. *I can't let her go that easily.* "I have something to say," Peter said, getting down onto one knee. The speech that he had memorized to propose to Mary Jane—the speech he never got to say—came flooding through his mind. "As I look into your eyes tonight . . . the reason I've asked you here . . ."

Mary Jane turned her face away so that Peter couldn't see her tears. "Please, Peter," she begged.

But Peter wouldn't stop. He wouldn't be interrupted, not again. ". . . because I see something beautiful inside you, and you see something beautiful inside me . . ."

Mary Jane couldn't bear it. "Just leave me alone!" she cried. She was crying openly now. The tears flowed as she ran away, leaving Peter alone in the park with his peonies.

CHAPTER 9

Peter lay on his bed, miserable. He couldn't stop thinking about Mary Jane.

What had happened? Why didn't she want to talk about it?

He knew that he had been out of line when he kissed Gwen. He knew that he hadn't been there for Mary Jane when she was sad. And he knew that he hadn't seemed grateful when Mary Jane had come over to comfort him about Uncle Ben.

But none of those seemed like good reasons

to break up with him. After all, people had argu-
ments all the time.

He didn't understand how he could have come
so close to marrying the woman of his dreams,
only to lose her before he got a chance to propose. Her face popped into his mind—the
unhappy look she had given him at the restaurant. More than anything, he wished he knew
what was the matter. He wanted to help Mary
Jane, but he didn't know how.

I don't even know how to help myself, Peter
thought. He felt as though an invisible hand was
squeezing his heart. *I just wish I could make this
horrible feeling go away. . . .*

Rolling over, his eyes landed on the trunk.

No. Don't touch that suit. It will change you. . . .

Well, maybe I want *to be different*, Peter
thought. *Besides, things can't get any worse
than they are now.*

Sitting up, he leaned over and flipped open the
top of the trunk. He reached in and pulled out the
black suit.

Just touching the fabric made him feel better,

stronger, and more in control.

Good, he thought as he ran his hands over the smooth black surface. *This is just what I need.*

I'll just wear it for a little while, he promised himself. *Just until I feel better.*

Peter was practically strutting as he walked through Manhattan later that day. With the new suit underneath his clothes, Peter felt like he could do anything. He winked at a girl who smiled at him. The black suit was working its magic, giving him extra energy, making him feel like he was burning with the radiance of a star. *Nothing can stop me now,* he thought as he walked past a newsstand. . . .

And stopped in his tracks.

SPIDER-MAN, THIEF! blared the front page of the *Daily Bugle.* Below was a photograph of Spider-Man in his new black suit—robbing a bank.

Peter felt as though the ground had dropped out from beneath his feet.

That never happened! Peter thought as he

gaped at the photograph. When he looked care-fully, he noticed that the photo looked familiar. It had been doctored. It was actually *two* photo-graphs. They had been put together to make it look like Spider-Man was a thief.

And I can prove it, Peter thought. *Because one of those photos is mine!*

But who would put a fake photo on the front page?

He looked down at the credit. "Eddie Brock," the name read.

Of course.

Peter's fingers clamped into a fist. *Brock,* he thought. J.J. Jameson had said that anyone who brought him a photo exposing Spider-Man would get the staff position at the *Bugle. Eddie wants that job so badly that he's willing to lie to get it,* Peter realized.

And he's willing to sell out Spider-Man.

Well, not this time, Peter thought as he turned away from the newsstand. *Eddie has been a thorn in my side since he arrived at the* Bugle, *but I'm not going to let him get away with this.*

He raced down the street—toward the *Daily Bugle* office. Spider-Man was going to get some justice from the press, for a change.

Holding out the newspaper, Peter confronted Eddie at his new desk—the one that he had received with the staff job. "Your picture's a fake."

Eddie sighed. "You're such a Boy Scout," he said with a carefree grin. "Give a guy a break."

With a lightning-fast move, Peter reached out and grabbed Eddie by his tie. Beneath Peter's clothes, the black suit pulsed with energy. Peter's muscles seemed to move with their own power as he shoved Eddie against a wall. A framed photo behind Eddie's head cracked under the pressure.

"Pete, please," Eddie begged. "If this gets out, there's not a paper in town that'll hire me." He thought about Gwen. He'd never be able to marry her without a job. "I'll lose everything."

Robbie Robertson, a *Daily Bugle* staff member, appeared at the door to Eddie's office to see if everything was okay. His eyes opened wide at what he saw—mild-mannered Peter Parker was threatening Eddie Brock!

"You should've thought about that earlier," Peter snarled at Eddie. He turned to Robbie and handed him a file. It was his own photograph—the one that Eddie had used to make Spider-Man look like a thief. "Show this to your editor," Peter told Robbie. "Tell him to check out his sources."

Peter strode out of the office. He knew that Eddie would be fired.

And he smiled.

Dressed in his black suit, Spider-Man crept silently into the Osborn mansion. He hadn't meant to wear it—but before he left his apartment, he decided to put it on under his clothes. Peter wanted to ask if Harry knew what was going on with Mary Jane. *Maybe he can help me figure out what to do,* Peter reasoned.

"What took you so long?" Harry asked. Only he wasn't Harry. It was the New Goblin, plotting away behind his mask, terrifyingly strong. His memories had returned—with a vengeance. Norman Osborn had reminded his son of who he really was, and now the New Goblin was ready for a taste of revenge.

"W-what?" Peter asked, stunned.

"I loved her, Pete," the New Goblin snarled as an image of Mary Jane's face flashed into his mind. "But you took her from me. You killed my father. And now you're going to pay." With a move like the crack of a whip, the New Goblin lunged at Spider-Man. Spider-Man fought back, but the New Goblin ripped through his webs like they were ribbons on a birthday present. Spider-Man grabbed his arms, and together they crashed through the full-length mirror that led to the Goblin's secret lair.

Fury pumped through the New Goblin's veins like fire. The black-suited Spider-Man lunged at his enemy with rage. He tackled the New Goblin and pounded his head against the floor. Spider-Man had him now—he could crush him.

"You gonna kill me like you killed my father?" The New Goblin sneered.

"Your father was a monster, and you know it!"

Spider-Man shouted in the villain's face. It gave him a cruel sort of joy to finally tell the truth. He had been protecting his friend for too long. "He tried to stab me in the back. I jumped out of the way." Leaning forward, he growled, "He never loved you."

The New Goblin writhed as though he had been stung with a hot flame. "My father loved me!" he cried, pain in his voice.

"He despised you," Spider-Man spat. "You were an embarrassment." Peter could hardly believe the words that he heard himself saying. He was doing everything he could to hurt his friend.

With a desperate move, the New Goblin reached for a pumpkin bomb and tossed it at Spider-Man. But Spider-Man was too quick—he shot it back just as the bomb went off.

It exploded near the side of Harry's face. His hands flew to his head as he let out a cry of surprise and pain. Turning, he caught sight of himself in the jagged glass of the broken mirror. What he saw there made him scream.

Spider-Man turned back to Harry. "Let me help

you!" Peter cried. "You have to go to the hospital!"

"Get away!" Harry shouted. "Get out of here!"

Peter didn't have a choice. He pulled on his black mask and swung away from Harry's mansion.

Peter leaned against a wall in the hallway of his dingy apartment building, the pay phone receiver gripped tightly in his hand. Just a few feet away, his patched-up door stood evenly on new hinges. After Peter's outburst, the landlord hadn't wasted any time in fixing it.

Being rude does have some *advantages,* Peter thought. Even so, his lock still wasn't working properly.

"Quite a specimen you left me, Parker." Dr. Connors's voice was raspy at the other end of the line.

"It is not unlike material found in that chondritic meteorite in the seventies," Peter's professor went on. Peter knew from his class that chondritic meteorites were made of small spheres that most scientists believed were formed by drops of liquid.

That would mean that the goo was very old—and from outer space. "But this material is an entire organism," Dr. Connors went on.

Organism? Peter thought, *as in a live being?* "It's living?" Peter asked.

"Even sentient," Dr. Connors said.

"It can think?" Peter couldn't believe his ears. *That black goo on my Spider-Man suit was a living, thinking thing? How could that be?* A chill went through his body.

"And it's clever," Dr. Connors went on. "Manipulates its host like a parasite. Can even change the host's behavior."

Peter bit his lip. *Change the host's behavior . . . like the black suit has changed mine.* An uneasy feeling grew in his stomach.

"I'd stay away from it," Dr. Connors advised. "It could be dangerous."

Images shot through his mind—hurting Harry with the bomb, turning Sandman to mud, shoving Eddie against the wall. *He's right,* Peter thought. *The suit is manipulating me, making me do what*

it wants instead of what I want. I should stay away from it.

He glanced back at his fixed door.

I'm just not sure that I want to.

Aunt May sat on the couch in her apartment, staring straight ahead. Peter wondered what she was thinking, but he couldn't read the emotions on her face. "How did he die?" Aunt May asked finally.

"Spider-Man did it," Peter said. He had just finished telling her about Sandman, and how the city didn't have anything to fear from him anymore. "I thought you'd be happy," Peter said. "I'm happy."

Aunt May looked sharply at her nephew. She was never happy to hear about anyone's death, not even that of a dangerous criminal, and she didn't think that Peter should be, either. There was nothing about it that sounded like justice to her ears. She knew that Peter felt strongly about crime and criminals ever since his uncle died, and she didn't blame him. But Aunt May knew that there was a difference between justice and vengeance. "Your uncle wouldn't want you living one second of your life with revenge in your heart," Aunt May told Peter sternly. "It's like poison." She looked him straight in the eye. "It can take us over. Before you know it, it turns us into something ugly."

Peter thought about that. He knew that his aunt was right, but he couldn't help his feelings. And the fact was that Sandman was gone, and Peter was happy about it.

That was just the truth.

CHAPTER 10

Peter laughed as he stepped through the door to the Jazz Room with Gwen on his arm. He had asked her on a date earlier that afternoon. *Time to move on with my life*, Peter had decided. *I can't just sit around moping over Mary Jane. I need to go out and do something.*

Gwen was looking particularly gorgeous, and the two of them had been having a wonderful evening. They'd laughed all through dinner and had really enjoyed themselves. Now it was time to move on to the main event.

So this is where Mary Jane is working, Peter thought as he surveyed the dingy club. No wonder she's feeling depressed. This place is a dump.

"Great idea, Pete," Gwen chirped as they walked to a table near the stage. "I never put you and jazz together."

Peter flashed her a smile. *Neither did I*, he thought. *Then again, I'm not really here for the jazz.*

Just then, the band finished their song and the trumpet player stepped up to the microphone. "Let's hear from you, Mary Jane," he said in his deep, bass voice.

Gwen blinked in surprise as Mary Jane put down her cocktail tray and hurried toward the stage. "Isn't that Mary Jane?" Gwen whispered to Peter. "Your old girlfriend?" She gave him a sympathetic look.

"Wild, huh?" Peter smiled dryly.

"Would you rather go someplace else?" Gwen asked, squeezing his arm.

Peter gave his head a quick shake. "I can handle it."

But just as Mary Jane was about to sing,

Peter leaped up onto the stage.

"Peter?" Mary Jane asked as he began to play the piano. She took a step back from the microphone in surprise, moving out of the spotlight.

Peter ignored her. "I'd like to dedicate this to a special lady out there," he said, grabbing the microphone. Very deliberately, he looked past Mary Jane . . . and toward Gwen. "A very special lady," he added, his voice suggestive.

Frozen in her seat, Gwen blushed. She barely knew Peter. *Why was he acting this way?*

The band picked up the beat as Peter began to play the piano. His fingers danced over the keys, punching out lively music. Once they were playing in time to his rhythm, Peter leaped onto the dance floor. Under his clothes, the black suit made him graceful and elegant—the same way it allowed him to play the piano with ease. He spun Gwen onto the floor and lowered her into a dip. But just as he was about to kiss her, Gwen pushed him away.

"That was for her, wasn't it?" Gwen demanded, her voice shaking with rage. "That's why you brought me here." She turned to Mary

Jane, who was staring at the scene in shock. "I'm so very sorry," Gwen said just before she walked out of the club.

Peter watched her go. He didn't feel bad about using her, though. After all, he'd come here to get revenge on Mary Jane, and he'd gotten it. He just hoped that she was feeling as horrible as she'd made him feel. . . .

The manager came over and asked Peter to leave, but he refused. Then the bouncer approached. He was enormous—easily twice Peter's size. But when he got near, Peter flipped him over onto his back. The black suit made it feel as easy as flipping a card.

Once he tossed the bouncer, the club erupted. It was chaos—almost every guy in the club jumped into the fight. Everyone was trying to stop Peter, but no one could. He was too strong, too fast, too nimble. He took on seven men at once, and they all ended up fighting each other.

Nothing can stop me! Peter thought as he fought off one person after another. *Nothing! These people are like insects compared to me!*

Finally, Mary Jane stepped forward to try to stop Peter. *He's acting crazy*, she thought. *I have to calm him down*. Stepping down from the stage, her hand reached for him.

Without thinking, Peter grabbed her, too.

His eyes widened when he saw what he had done. In the club, everything stopped. Nobody moved.

Mary Jane stared at Peter. She looked like she couldn't believe what she was seeing. "What's happened to you?" she whispered.

Peter felt sick as he looked at Mary Jane. *Why am I acting this way? I love Mary Jane!* Shame washed over him like a wave. "I don't know," Peter admitted, miserable.

In the fight, his collar had come loose. The black fabric of the Spider-Man suit was visible at his neck.

"It's the suit," Mary Jane said.

No, Peter thought as he ran out of the jazz club. *No!*

But he knew it was true. It *was* the suit. It was the black goo. It was making him . . . evil.

Feeling desperate, Peter ran down the block. He didn't know where he was going—he just ran.

His feet pounded on the pavement as he dashed through the city.

There, he thought as he caught sight of an ancient ruin of a church. Light flickered dimly through the beautiful broken stained-glass windows.

I need the highest point, he thought, searching for the stairs. *I have to get out of sight!* Finally, he found them. Taking the steps two at a time, he climbed to the top and found himself surrounded by enormous bells.

The bell tower.

I have to get rid of this suit, he thought, yanking off his shirt. *I have to get rid of it once and for all!*

But when he reached for the black fabric, it wouldn't come off. Peter tried again, but the black suit was stuck to his skin, almost as though it was glued in place—it was like it had become part of him.

Oh, no, Peter thought. *I can't take it off! I'll be wild and evil and powerful. . . .*

Forever . . .

Happiness flickered in his chest. The truth was, he didn't want to get rid of the suit. Not really. And now he didn't have to. . . .

Mary Jane's face burst into his mind, and he saw the hurt expression she had worn in the jazz club. His heart ached. *I can't do this anymore*, he decided. *I have to get rid of this suit. It's trying to make me keep it, but I won't. I won't!*

Screaming in pain, he dug his fingernails into the black fabric and ripped, tearing the suit from his flesh. It wouldn't come off.

Peter staggered backward, bumping one of the enormous bells.

Gong!

At the sound of the bell, the black suit roiled across his skin. Peter gaped as the suit came off in clumps, and bits of oozing goo dropped to the floorboards. He rang another bell and more goo oozed off of him, dripping between the cracks, and down through the ceiling to the floor below, where Eddie Brock sat staring up at the spectacle of Peter Parker tearing his black spider suit away from his body. His mouth dropped open in shock. *Peter Parker is Spider-Man? The two people who ruined my life are really one?*

Eddie shook his head as the pieces slowly began to fit together. This explained everything. How Peter was the only person—besides himself—who ever managed to get photos of the webbed one. And why he had taken Eddie's fake photograph so personally. *Of course. Of course!* Eddie thought.

Eddie was stunned by the scene above him, unable to believe his eyes. Ever since Peter had exposed the truth about his phony photo, Eddie had been keeping an eye on him. And he had plenty of time to follow him everywhere—after all, he didn't have a job anymore. Gwen had announced that she didn't want to see him, so he didn't have a girlfriend anymore. He didn't have *anything* anymore—nothing but a wish for revenge.

When he had seen Peter walk into the jazz club with Gwen earlier, Eddie had stumbled away to the church down the street. Eddie had actually been praying for a way to get back at Peter when a bit of black goo plopped onto his head.

Above him, Peter writhed in pain as he struggled with the black suit. More black goo oozed off of him, and a piece splattered on the back of Eddie's hand.

Then another bit dripped onto his face and onto his tongue.

Lightning ripped through Eddie's body. The black goo made him feel as though he was on fire. His muscles stretched and flexed, growing with the power of the black ooze. Eddie grinned madly.

From the bell tower, Peter let out a wild scream as he fought with the suit.

With the black venom on his tongue, Eddie screamed, too, as the black goo took over his body, transforming him. The two voices blended together, rising up into the New York City night.

Steam trailed from the shower, seeped beyond the bathroom door and trickled into Peter's apartment. He sighed under the hot water as he washed the last traces of the ooze from his body. His skin was pink and raw, but for the first time in weeks, Peter felt clean.

Meanwhile, the door to Peter's apartment swung open silently on its new hinges. With his new black skin, Eddie had easily slipped into the lobby when no one was looking. And since the lock on Peter's door still wasn't working, Eddie had no trouble letting himself in.

I could kill him right here, Eddie thought as he looked around Peter's grimy apartment. *I'll just wait until he gets out of the shower and surprise him. But that would be too easy. . . .*

Eddie was tired of taking the easy way out. No, he wanted to show Peter that he and the rest of the world had underestimated Eddie Brock. *Peter thinks he's so great,* Eddie thought bitterly as he caught sight of the spider suit in Peter's closet. *Spider-Man is just so perfect, isn't he? But he isn't the only hero in town anymore.* Eddie wanted Peter to know that he was powerful, too. This black stuff that Peter had tossed away—it was making Eddie feel amazing, like he could climb mountains . . . or crush them.

No, I won't kill him now, Eddie decided. *I want*

to kill him in public, with the world watching. Because I don't just want to bring down Peter Parker. Who cares about him? I want to bring down Spider-Man.

Still, he wasn't sure that he could do it alone. Taking on Spider-Man would require a plan . . . and maybe some help. Eddie thought he knew where he could get that help. As for the plan. . .

Eddie looked at the photograph at Peter's bedside. It was a picture of a beautiful red-haired girl. He recognized her as the waitress in the jazz club—the one Peter had made himself a fool for. He must feel pretty strongly about her. *It shouldn't be too hard to find out her name*, Eddie thought, smiling to himself.

And then the spider will become the prey.

CHAPTER 11

Flint Marko stood in the light of a streetlamp, looking up at the yellow glow from his daughter's room. It hurt him to know that Penny was up there—sick—and that he couldn't be with her. He still hadn't stolen enough money to save her. When Flint had checked in with Dr. Wallace, the doctor had assured him that he was working as quickly as he could. But he still hadn't found a cure.

But that's going to change, Flint thought as he watched the window. *I'm going to get a cure for Penny. The doctor and I . . . we're going to save her.* "I'm your father," he whispered, "watching you all the time. I got you in my heart." He swallowed hard, fighting the lump in his throat. "I'm gonna find a way for you to be strong."

"Ah, the family," said a voice.

Looking over, Flint saw a black-clad figure standing nearby. It was Eddie Brock.

"Do I know you?" Flint growled.

"I'm the enemy of your enemy," Eddie said.

Flint didn't know what that meant, so Eddie had to explain that both he and Flint had something in common—they wanted to get rid of Spider-Man. And while having an enemy in common didn't exactly make them friends, it could make them allies in the fight of the century.

"I just want to tie him down somewhere," Flint said. "Keep him off my neck."

Eddie grinned. Could anyone be a more perfect ally than Sandman—the person who had almost defeated Spider-Man single-handedly? *Spider-Man can't possibly handle us both. We'll finish him in no time.* Eddie wrapped an arm around Flint's shoulder. "Then follow me."

Televisions across the city announced the news—Sandman had taken a hostage. A taxi dangled from a black web attached to a crane. Live footage streamed from the site as Eddie—now known as Venom—wrote a dark message in his web, for the media to see. It read: STOP US IF YOU CAN. It was a dare for the city's hero.

"This is a suicide mission for Spider-Man," one newscaster observed.

As Peter Parker watched the scene, he had to agree.

As though she were standing beside him, Peter heard Mary Jane's words. "We all need help sometimes, Peter," she had said.

Well, I need some help right now, Peter thought. *If only I had an ally . . .*

But who in the world could help Spider-Man?

Harry sat in a darkened room, watching the hostage crisis unfold in the blue light of his television set. He had called a private doctor to tend his wounds. The doctor said that he would heal, but he told Harry that his face may never look completely normal.

Peter Parker strikes again, Harry thought bitterly.

Harry was absorbed in these thoughts when a silent figure crept in through the window.

"Why don't you come in, Pete?" Harry snarled. "I guess you will. You always manage to do whatever you want."

Peter crept out of the shadows. "Harry," he said gently. "They have M.J."

Harry blinked at the television. *Mary Jane?* he thought. *Of course . . . it all makes sense. If you want to catch Spider-Man, you have to bait the trap.* His stomach twisted anxiously, half in fear, half in anger.

"I can't take them both," Peter said quietly as he stood in the center of the Osborn living room. "Not by myself."

He could barely look at Harry. His old friend's face was twisted and mangled, disfigured by the pumpkin bomb. *I did that,* Peter thought, his shame making him sick. *I did that to my best friend, and now I'm standing here asking him for help.*

But he didn't have a choice. He had to try. "I need your help, Harry," Peter begged.

What's the point of helping Mary Jane? Harry thought. *She'll just go running right back to Peter.* The muscles along Harry's jawline worked as he ground his teeth in rage. "If you want to save M.J., you're going to have to do it yourself," he snarled. "Get out."

Peter was disappointed, but hardly surprised, as he turned to go.

Once the door had clicked closed behind Peter, Harry let out a cry. He held his head, struggling with the thoughts that raced through his mind. *I should help him*, he thought.

No, I should help the others—Sandman and that one in the black suit. I should help them defeat Spider-Man.

It was what his father would have wanted, after all.

But Harry couldn't make himself move. He didn't know what to do.

He just didn't know.

🕷 🕷 🕷

Seventy-five stories up over the city, a cab dangled unsteadily in a black web. It swayed back and forth like a pendulum at every breath of wind, making Mary Jane feel sick. "Why do they always come after me?" she wailed from the cab's backseat. "Do I have the word 'bait' stamped on my forehead?" She was frightened, but she was furious, too. It just wasn't right! Some people never got taken hostage—and she had to be a hostage practically once a year!

Snap!

Mary Jane screamed as the car plunged five stories down. One of the webs had broken, nearly sending the cab crashing to the pavement—with Mary Jane in it. Other junk was stuck in the web nearby—including a heavy Dumpster filled with concrete and metal beams. It was above her. *If that tips*, Mary Jane thought, *it's all over*.

There was a gentle thud as Spider-Man landed on the hood of the cab.

Mary Jane's heart fluttered and she forgot all about how furious she had been with Peter the night before. He was here—and she had never been so happy to see anyone in her entire life.

"Peter," Mary Jane said as he peered at her through the windshield, "they're never going to let you out of here alive."

Peter knew it was true. Venom and Sandman hadn't taken Mary Jane hostage for nothing. They wanted Spider-Man.

Roar!

A furious sound bellowed from Venom as he swung toward them, kicking Spider-Man through the windshield. Glass shattered over Mary Jane, covering her in dangerous shards.

Spider-Man clung to the trunk of the car as Venom climbed toward him. He was an oozing mass of black, changing faces. . . .

Suddenly, the goo receded a bit, revealing Eddie's face. "Hiya, pal," he said with sinister cheer. "Remember me?"

Spider-Man gaped at the thing before him. It was Eddie Brock, but at the same time it wasn't. Now that he wasn't wearing the suit, it was clear how it took people over, and it was an ugly sight. "You've got to take off that suit!" Peter cried. "It'll—"

Venom kicked Spider-Man in the face, and he lost his grip. Falling away from the cab, Peter dropped ten stories. The ground rushed up to meet him, but Venom broke his fall. He trapped Spider-Man's wrist, binding him to an enormous black web. Then he spun a web around his other wrist.

Spider-Man was helpless, flat on his back in a giant web. His arms and legs were spread. The pavement below seemed far away as he struggled against the black web. But the more he fought, the more the bonds at his wrists grew tighter.

Sneering, Venom kneed him in the ribs. The wind knocked out of him, Peter choked. Then— before he could react—Venom ripped off Spider-Man's mask. He looked Peter right in the face.

Now is my moment, Venom thought. *I have Spider-Man right where I want him!*

With a heavy metallic creak, the Dumpster shifted toward Mary Jane.

"What do you want, Eddie?" Peter cried. Time was running out. He had to act fast.

"To be honest," Venom said cheerfully, Eddie's face showing again, "I want to kill you."

The words chilled Peter to the bone. He knew that Venom could kill him, and as long as Eddie was wearing that suit, there was no way to get through to him. "We can find a way to settle this," Peter said. He struggled to keep his voice calm.

"You're so right," Eddie chirped, bringing his finger to his lips. "I was thinking . . . humiliation. Just as you humiliated me . . . but televised." He gestured toward the street, where TV camera crews from every station in town were gathered to watch the show. "Spider-Man screws up, and sweet little Mary Jane dies." Eddie's voice turned dark. "You made me lose my girl, now I'm going to make you lose yours."

Below them, Gwen shouted up through a bull-horn, begging Eddie to come to his senses. But Eddie ignored her. It was too late now. Besides, he didn't care about Gwen much anymore. He had the black suit. And he had his revenge. That was all he really wanted.

The Dumpster tilted, dropping dangerous debris toward the cab with Mary Jane in it. *Bang! Bang! Bang!* Cinder blocks, concrete slabs, and steel brackets rained down on the taxi, ripping through the webs that held it in place.

A piece of sheet metal fell from the Dumpster and sliced through the web where Peter was trapped.

Both he and Venom fired webs—but neither was quick enough. They each hit the ground hard.

Groaning with effort, Peter pulled his mask back over his face before the television crews could film his real identity.

Smash!

Sandman hit him with a hammer blow. Spider-Man stumbled backward, staggering under the weight of the blast.

Slam!

Venom's fist smashed into him, whipping Spider-Man back toward Sandman, who hit him again.

With a horrifying groan, the Dumpster tore through the web, screaming toward the pavement as it fell.

Crash!

A corner of the Dumpster caught the side of the cab, and the taxi lolled onto its side like a beached whale. Thrown by the impact, Mary Jane cried out as she smacked against the driver's-side door. A scream caught in her throat as the solid metal gave way beneath her. The door popped open and her legs plunged into the empty space below.

Without thinking, Mary Jane grabbed the steering wheel. She struggled to keep her grip as she dangled sixty stories above Peter.

"M.J.!" Peter shouted.

Wind howled as a sandstorm grew and swirled around him. Sand pulled together, forming a solid mass as large as a mountain. It writhed in the air with powerful muscles, sweeping up steam shovels, concrete, and all sorts of debris in its path. The entire construction site seemed to whistle in the wind.

Looking up, Peter saw that Sandman had grown. He was more than a storm, more than a man—he was five hundred tons of furious sand, and he was on the move.

Stomp!

Stomp!

Stomp!

Sandman careened forward, crushing everything in his path as his giant feet crashed forward
on the pavement.

Peter dodged away as Sandman's enormous
hands reached for him. With a grunt of effort,
Spider-Man shot a web at the giant villain—but
Venom leaped between them, slicing the spider
thread. He thrust a powerful kick at Spider-Man,
who received the horrible blow with agonizing pain.

Above the battle, Mary Jane's fingers slipped
from the smooth vinyl of the taxi's steering wheel.
No! she thought as she desperately tried to hang
on. But it was no use. She couldn't keep her grip
any longer. . . .

Mary Jane screamed as her hand slipped
from the steering wheel, her arms flailing wildly
as she fell through the air. But Venom's sticky
strands stretched around her as she reached the
very bottom of the black web. She was stuck.
Now she had nowhere left to fall—nowhere but
the hard street below.

Terrified, Mary Jane looked up. Above her, the

cab dangled uncertainly. Any minute, it would tear loose, and when it did, they would both fall. The taxi would land on top of her, crushing her against the pavement. She needed help, but she couldn't speak. Fear kept a lump in her throat the size of an orange, silencing her voice.

"Kill him now!" Venom spat as he reached his hands around Spider-Man's neck, crushing his throat. Choking, Spider-Man flailed at Venom's hands in an effort to tear himself free. But Venom was too strong. His grip was like a vise. Spider-Man kept fighting—he had to find a way to save Mary Jane!

Sandman towered above them, ready for the final blow.

The black web stretched and groaned under the weight of the taxi. . . .

With a shout, Spider-Man leaped, firing his webs at Mary Jane. Venom leaped after him, but he wasn't fast enough. He slammed against a concrete balcony, high atop a skyscraper.

Spider-Man shoved Mary Jane out of the way of the giant Sandman, who tottered toward her on legs the size of cranes.

Slam!

Sandman's fist blasted through the side of the building, sending chunks of concrete and metal flying. He swiped at Spider-Man, but the hero was too nimble—he dodged out of the way.

But Sandman didn't back away. He curled his tree-like fingers into a fist and clenched, ready to bring the hammer down onto Spider-Man.

But Venom struck first. Eddie Brock strode forward on powerful legs, his taut muscles rippling beneath his black suit. A steel pipe gleamed dangerously in his hands.

Slam!

Venom blasted Spider-Man with the pipe, cracking him across the ribs. Peter groaned in agony, staggering backward from the force of the blow.

Venom toyed with the pipe as though it was a baton. With an elegant flip, he turned it over so that the blunt end was at the bottom. The other end was sharp as a spike, and pointed directly at Spider-Man.

"Don't give in to the anger, Eddie," Spider-Man

warned, coughing. He struggled to inhale—every breath was agony. "It just feeds the suit. It wants you to hate." Peter knew that there was only one way to make the suit powerless, and that was to keep your emotions in check. It was a lesson he had learned the hard way. "Give it up!"

Venom smiled cruelly. How boringly predictable for Spider-Man to try to get him to give up the suit. *Of course that's what he wants*, Eddie reasoned. *He's jealous! He's envious that there is a new hero in town. That goody-two-webs can't bear to share the limelight*, Eddie thought. *Well, he's about to learn a lesson—the hard way.* "How can I give this up?" Eddie demanded. "Finally, I'm somebody. Look at them down there," he said as he gestured to the desperate crowd that had gathered at the edge of the construction site, "waiting for my next move." He grinned. "I *like* being bad," he said cheerfully. "It makes me happy."

In a flash, Venom charged at Spider-Man, but Spider-Man fought back. With a deft move, he lunged at the pipe, snatching it from Venom's hands. He only meant to disarm him, but Venom fought back. The pipe twisted into an awkward angle, plunging into Venom's stomach.

Eddie gasped for breath, looking down at the pipe in surprise. The black muck that had slithered over him began to boil and recede, revealing Eddie's face.

Thank goodness it's gone, Spider-Man thought. Killed forever.

Looking at the black goo, Peter remembered the clanging of the church bells as he pulled the black suit from his own flesh. The black ooze had been unstoppable . . . except that night in the bell tower. When the bells began to toll, the black goo had disappeared, evaporated, as though the noise itself was destroying it. . . .

Overhead was a crane holding a sling. In a flash, Peter flung a web at the sling. With a vicious yank, Spider-Man sent hundreds of steel rods raining down.

Bong! Gong! Clang!

As the rods fell, they clanged against metal girders, ringing out over the city like bells.

The black ooze let out a hideous scream of

agony. But the noise did not stop or even slow down. Instead, the sonic vibrations joined together, creating a powerful force.

The snake-like ooze shrieked as the vibrations split it apart, sending it slithering away in all directions.

The city was safe again—thanks to Spider-Man.

"For I must have you or no one," Mary Jane sang into the microphone as couples swayed on the dance floor at the jazz club. "And so I'm through with love."

Peter heard the music halfway up the block as he made his way to the tiny club. There was now a large photo of Mary Jane in the window, right next to a glowing review. Peter smiled at the words. NOT TO BE MISSED, the critic had written. A NEW, ENCHANTING SONGBIRD HAS FLOWN INTO TOWN.

Enchanting is right, Peter thought as he pulled open the heavy wooden door. *That's the perfect word for M.J.*

Mary Jane smiled as Peter walked into the club, but she didn't stumble over her song. Peter waited until she had finished, then moved to the dance floor. "Dance?" he mouthed, just as the band struck up the opening bars of "Falling in Love."

Peter looked down into Mary Jane's green eyes. "We have a lot to talk about," he said.

Mary Jane put her finger to his lips. "Let's not talk about the relationship," she told him. "Just shut up and dance."

So he did.